THE LADY MAK

Morgan Ashbury

MENAGE AMOUR

Siren Publishing, Inc.
www.SirenPublishing.com

A SIREN PUBLISHING BOOK
IMPRINT: Ménage Amour

THE LADY MAKES THREE
Copyright © 2009 by Morgan Ashbury

ISBN-10: 1-60601-466-8
ISBN-13: 978-1-60601-466-0

First Printing: June 2009

Cover design by Jinger Heaston
All cover art and logo copyright © 2009 by Siren Publishing, Inc.

Printed in the U.S.A.

PUBLISHER
Siren Publishing, Inc.
www.SirenPublishing.com

DEDICATION

To my Sister Sirens Emma and Lara, for believing I could; and to James Angus, who kept me honest.

THE LADY MAKES THREE

MORGAN ASHBURY
Copyright © 2009

Chapter 1

Naked arousal bucked her from sleep to wakefulness in a single heartbeat.

Maddy Dalton tossed the blankets aside and dropped her feet to the floor. Breath choppy, head bowed, she struggled to rein in her horniness. Moonlight spilled through the window, soft light pooling on every surface, making the perspiration on her arms and breasts glisten. Another kind of moisture altogether slicked her sex.

Bare wisps of the dream remained, phantom images teasing of their presence and even though she knew it was a mistake, she struggled to recall them, see them, *feel* them.

Masculine flesh rippling with muscle. A touch. A taste. As these hints kissed her mind, Maddy's nerve endings tingled in remembered pleasure. Closing her eyes, she slid, supine, back onto the tumbled sheets, back toward the dream.

As her hand reached down and stroked her feminine flesh, it was joined by another, masculine one. The caress of work-roughened fingers over the fullness of her breasts peaked her nipples, turning them to pebbled points. A masculine grunt of smug pleasure preceded forefinger and thumb capturing one nipple, pinching hard.

The pain, sharply exquisite, bowed her off the bed. She whimpered as arousal spiked higher, sending tiny lightning bolts from her core along every inch of her skin. Helpless against the sensation, she spread her legs wide—invitation and surrender combined. Strong fingers found sensitive folds, delved into moisture, reaching deep. Stoke after stroke stoked fires, fed the hunger, but somehow never quite sated it. Maddy stretched her body taut, rolling her hips to meet the thrusts, striving higher and harder until she nearly cried out in desperation. Needing more, craving a strong touch everywhere, her wish was granted as hands caressed and claimed breasts and belly, while fingers skittered along the crack of her ass, teased and yet continued to plunge within her, all at the same time.

It burst, a sharp and bright bubble of orgasm, some but not all, good, but not good enough, never quite good enough.

Tiny shivers coursed through her. Limp, exhausted, her right hand stayed where it sprawled nearly lifeless, nestled on top of the curls that covered her sex.

Her eyes flicked to the bedside clock even as she sensed she had no time left to return to sleep. No time left to think about the aching emptiness that lived inside her—had lived inside her for what seemed like forever. Dawn would be breaking soon, the dawn of a new day. It would be another in a string of new days that never seemed to change, an infinite dawning of sameness that made up her existence. Get over it, Maddy thought as she moved her head back and forth on her pillow. She had an existence, she didn't have a life.

Annoyed at the maudlin turn of her thoughts, Maddy once more put her feet on the floor, this time completing the momentum and getting out of bed. She needed a shower—hot, steamy and now. Blistering, beating water would chase useless fantasies and even more useless self-pity down the drain, where they belonged. She had to get a move on.

The ranch needed her. Always, the ranch needed her.

* * * *

Dawn crept toward the horizon, and the world outside the window appeared a little less dark than just a few minutes before. The scent of sausage and flapjacks filled the air, mingling with the ever present aroma of coffee. For the residents of the Circle D ranch, three hundred miles southwest of Denver Colorado, another day had already begun.

The screen door banged shut and Lucas Calhoun took his time looking up from his coffee. He knew who'd just come into the bunkhouse, of course. He had, in fact, been waiting for her. That's why he took his time, turned his head only after one of the other hands greeted the new arrival. Where Maddy was concerned, he found it harder each day to keep his emotions in check.

"Morning, boss," Bill called out, his voice cigarette-hoarse.

"Morning, Bill. Men."

Maddy's greeting sounded a little strained. Lucas couldn't keep his eyes from drinking in her presence like a parched man. Shadows darkened the delicate flesh under her eyes and tiredness draped over her slender frame, a weariness that seemed heavier now than it had six months before when she'd not only been running the Circle D but caring for her ailing father as well.

But old Robert Dalton had been gone these last few months, and Maddy's load should have been easier for her to bear. He knew what a strain the sire had placed on the filly. It bothered him she looked so battered. He wished he had the right to go to her, take her into his arms and simply soothe the burden away.

He didn't have that right, more, he would likely never have it and sure as hell didn't deserve to, either. Sensing eyes on him, he looked up and into the clear blue-eyed gaze of the ranch's newest official employee and honorary prodigal son, Chase Reynolds.

Telling himself the emotions that fired to life within him at Chase's close scrutiny were merely discomfort at being caught wool gathering, Lucas reached for the coffee pot Bill had set on the table and poured himself another cup. Then he poured some of the brew into the cup at the empty spot next to him as well.

"Come have some joe, Maddy, and tell us what you want done today."

Maddy pulled out the chair next to him and sat down at the same time Chase settled himself directly across from them both.

"Thanks, Luc. Settling in all right, Chase? Taken a few walks down memory lane, yet?"

Maddy's tone held a slight edge of teasing, the standard tone used by most everyone at the dinner table.

Chase had officially been added to the staff a couple of days before, but he was no stranger to Lucas, Maddy, or the ranch. A quiet boy of ten when his father, Vic Reynolds, had been hired on some twenty years before, Chase had grown up on the Circle D. It wasn't a usual kind of thing, to find a ranch hand traveling the country looking for work with a child in tow. But Chase's mother had just died the winter before, and there'd been no other family for the boy to go to.

Since Lucas had the entire foreman's house to himself, and because the bunkhouse didn't qualify as a good environment for a child, he'd invited Vic and Chase to move in with him. Vic had been an okay worker, though not an industrious one. Lucas might have fired his ass if he hadn't taken such a liking to young Chase.

When Chase turned sixteen, Vic had up and quit. No one much cared if they saw the back of the father, but they all regretted Chase's departure.

Now he'd returned, a man fully grown, and from what Lucas had seen so far strong of back and smart of brain.

Lucas turned his focus back to the conversation.

"Settled in just fine, Maddy, thanks. Place hasn't changed much, that's for sure. Well, except I can't go up to the house and play checkers with Mr. D. That used to be one of the highlights of my day, growing up here. I was sorry to hear he'd passed."

Lucas noted the look of gratitude on Maddy's face for Chase's kind words. Robert Dalton had been a son-of-a-bitch to most people, including Maddy. But she'd loved the old bastard anyway. And for reasons the old man had never explained, he'd taken a liking to Chase. Lucas secretly suspected that he looked on the young boy as a second chance, in some ways. He'd only ever had one child— Maddy—and no doubt some part of him had pined for a son to carry on after him. *Stupid bastard.* Maddy had grown into a finer person, a harder worker, and a better daughter than Dalton had had any right to expect.

Lucas waited for the platter of sausages and jacks that Bill had just set down to be passed around. Bill Campbell—who pitched in with the horses when he wasn't cooking—himself and Chase made up the 'originals' on the ranch, if such a term applied. The other two men, Pat and Charlie, had hired on about three years before. In the busy season, Maddy would take on extra men, temporary workers. There never seemed to be a shortage of cowboys drifting by, looking for a few weeks work. Branding season had just passed, and an early heat wave had struck. The five of them plus Maddy made for plenty of hands to get things done until the fall.

"I rode passed the hay field yesterday. Crop looks to have taken a good hold. If the weather gods are kind, we should end up with plenty to feed the horses over winter."

Lucas tuned in to ranch business. "Thought the same myself. I also thought that with Chase here now, it's not out of the question to run over to Gunnison for whatever supplies we need."

"Something wrong with the Seed & Feed in Marshville?" Chase asked.

"Nuthin' 'cepting that fancy pants Kevin Marsh thinking he's entitled to come round sniffin' at Miss Maddy." Bill's succinct explanation came filtered through a mouthful of food. Bill was a fine cook and a good hand, but had no table manners to speak of.

Lucas tried to interpret the sharp look Chase shot him just then. *Hell, I'm no good at that sort of thing, reading people's expressions.* He knew enough when someone spouted bullshit, and he could generally tell if someone became really pissed at him, but that spelled the limit of his people reading skills. And Kevin Marsh, in Lucas's estimation, was drowning in the former. He turned to look at Maddy as she began to fill Chase in.

"He took to visiting Dad about two months before he passed. Never could figure out why, but Dad seemed glad to have a visitor. Then, not long after the funeral, he came by one day, suddenly filled with ardor. When I told him I had no interest in dating him, he tried to tell me that he'd had a gentleman's agreement with Dad, who'd given his blessings to Marsh's marrying me and taking over running this ranch."

"Ain't no gentleman," Charlie said now. "Begging' your pardon, Maddy, I meant Marsh, not your pa."

Maddy's smile flashed quick and keen and lit up her entire face. The sight of it never failed to lift Lucas's spirits. He sensed Chase's penetrating gaze once more, and decided to ignore it.

"You've got that right," Maddy agreed with the man. Then she shrugged her shoulders as she finished her explanation for Chase. "I told him to go to hell. Since then whenever I've gone into town to get one thing or another we've needed, I've come away empty handed, because Marsh—who you may recall not only owns the only real estate business in Marshville but the Seed & Feed as well—claims whatever it is we want is 'out of stock'. The last time that happened, I asked Bert Smitherman, over at the Double Horseshoe Ranch to get the item for me instead. An hour later, same day, and what do you know, Marsh had it."

"What does he think he's going to achieve that way?" Chase asked, and he looked, not only to Maddy, but Lucas for his answer.

Lucas shrugged. "I don't think he's trying to achieve anything really. He's simply being a vindictive little bastard."

"That's my take too," Maddy said. "I'd just as soon avoid him in the near future, if we could. And we can, now. Lucas is right. Having an extra man around—and one I can count on at that—will make it possible to take the extra time when needed to run into Gunnison."

"Well, then. I'm very glad to be of service."

Chase had looked straight at Lucas when he'd said that, his words accompanied by a look that could have steamed ice. Lucas felt a strange tightening in his belly, noted the way his pulse kicked up. Swallowing hard, he looked away from the younger man, putting his attention on his empty plate even as he felt his cock begin to stir.

Lucas didn't remember having eaten his breakfast, but at the moment that seemed the least of his worries.

* * * *

Maddy tilted her head back, the water from her canteen hitting her square in the face, then running down the front of her t-shirt and onto her jeans. This heat wave was unusual for mid-May. But she'd worked through worse heat waves before with equanimity and couldn't understand why today's record temperature got to her so badly. *I'm just tired, that's all.*

Stopping the deluge with a quarter of the bottle to spare, Maddy brought the metal to her lips. As she drank, she scanned the area. Chase and Luc were both giving her a hand with this fence repair job. Lucas stood about a hundred yards to her right, his button-front shirt open, sweat beading on his chest. She watched as his gaze traced the path of the water on her own shirt, noted the look of interest and the quick darting-away of his eyes.

Someday I'm going to have myself a few stiff shots of whiskey for courage and attack that man. She couldn't deny that thoughts of Lucas, naked, had taken up residence in her mind on more than one occasion. She felt pretty sure the man viewed her the same way. She couldn't figure out why neither one of them had made a move on each other after all these years. About the same age as she, Lucas had been a part of her life since they'd been teenagers. Neither one of them had a significant other nor could be considered butt-ugly.

Damn it, she was lonely. Cry-herself-to-sleep-in-the-middle-of-the-night-sometimes lonely. She wanted someone in her life, someone who would respect her and hold her; who would be there when she needed him but wouldn't expect her to cater to him twenty-four seven. One thing she knew for certain: she really didn't want a husband. She didn't want the work, the worry or the responsibility of one.

She'd spent the last twelve years of her life caring for her father after he'd become sick. She'd had to make every decision, face every challenge, clear every hurdle, on her own, while catering to most every one of his needs. In other words, she'd filled the role of 'wife' of the household and had no desire to go there again.

Why the big deal in society about getting married, anyway? Her father had considered her lack of a husband to be her worst sin. Hell, marriage was nothing more than a vow, a promise and a piece of paper, none of which had any value at all, in most cases.

Chase stretched, catching Maddy's attention. He stood only a few feet away, directly in front of her by the open tail gate of the truck, and the expansive movement definitely snagged her interest. Obviously he'd tossed his t-shirt in deference to the heat and she couldn't help but notice and appreciate his well honed abs and pecs. She nearly jumped when his eyes met hers. His gaze bored into her. When he shifted his focus to her breasts, she felt a tingling response in the pit of her belly. Then his eyes met hers again and she had no trouble seeing the hunger in them. He tossed her a flirty grin and headed back to his piece of barbed wire.

Well, hell, now what? Was she so desperate to get laid that she could lust after two different men with an equal craving and at the same time? Images from her dream that very morning slithered across her mind. She'd brought those images back as she'd pleasured herself, and yes, in her imagining there sure as hell had been more than two male hands on her body as she'd come. Maddy turned her eyes away from the younger man as that reality hit home. Capping her canteen, she tossed it on the ground, pulled her gloves back on, and got back to working on the fence. She kept her hat brim down so she could look at both men without their catching her at it. Both worked quickly and efficiently as they attacked portions of the old boundary line. She saw Lucas turn his head toward Chase, but couldn't see the expression on her foreman's face. Then, a few minutes later, when she looked up again, she saw Chase treating the other man the same kind of look he'd just given her.

All right, that settles it. I've obviously got sex on the brain. She blamed that strange dream near dawn, which itself had likely just sprung—even if it had been a first, dreaming of two lovers at the same time—from her having neglected her body's needs for so long. It had been years since her last lover. Narrowing her eyes, she tried to think back…holy hell, the last man she'd had a relationship with was Tom Parker, and that had been nearly six years ago! It had also been a long time since she'd given herself a really good session with her vibrator.

Tom Parker had been a scratch in response to an itch, nothing more. Just as well seeing as the man hadn't stayed in the county very long after their half-hearted affair had begun. Her vibrator, now, she had no excuse there. She didn't even have to worry about anyone else being in the house with her anymore, either, interfering with her privacy. Maybe this weekend she'd have a nice long bubble bath, a couple glasses of wine, and see what she could do about taking care of her inner woman with Bob—her battery operated boyfriend.

Chapter 2

Chase Reynolds was hard.

Who wouldn't be after the afternoon he'd just spent? Throwing his discarded clothes onto his bed he walked, naked, into one of the two showers located in the bunkhouse. He turned on the spray and adjusted the heat while he turned everything over in his mind.

If he'd thought even for a moment that following his instincts and coming home to the Circle D had been a fool's journey, he could put that doubt to rest for good after this afternoon. The realization that he'd been right, and that his fondest dream had a hell of a good chance of becoming reality washed over him even more soothingly than the hot water did.

Chase had never considered himself an ambitious man. True, he'd attended college, gotten himself a degree in business management, and had worked for a few years for a major financial institution in New York. He'd shown a knack for making money, and had soon been dabbling in the high-stakes high-profit field of venture capitalism. But money and the desire to possess material goods had never driven him. Searching for his niche, he'd left Wall Street for a stint in law enforcement. But that hadn't really been for him, either.

The only thing he'd ever really wanted was a home and a place to belong.

Chase hadn't majored in psychology, but he understood himself, his dream, and where it stemmed from.

Neither of his parents had ever really wanted him. He'd lived with his mom after his dad had split when he'd been around three. But he'd spent a lot of time on his own, either fending for himself days on end while his mom went "out", or hiding under his bed when whichever sleaze bag she'd drag home would get hopped up on drugs or booze and want to use him as a punching bag.

After his mom had died, he'd gone to live with his dad. To give the old man credit, at least he'd stepped up to the plate and claimed him, rather than letting him languish in the system. But Victor Reynolds had no more desire to make a family and a home than his mother had.

It was perfect irony that only place Chase had ever felt at home had been a place he'd found thanks to his dad—right here on the Circle D, with Maddy and Lucas.

As the years away had passed and he thought back to his life here, he'd wondered in hindsight if the clues he thought he noticed when he'd been a confused teenager had been real, or just a case of transference. Coming back as an adult, one no longer confused, he'd paid attention. Approaching thirty, he knew himself and was perfectly comfortable in his self-awareness—and in his bi-sexuality. He loved women. He loved men. Sex, in Chase's estimation, had to be the greatest thrill in the world. But sex without the strings of emotion, without the structure of commitment, had gotten old. And when he thought about those three things together—sex, emotion, and commitment—he knew he'd had to come home.

Chase made quick work of rinsing off. It was early yet, not even six. Having spent the afternoon looking and wanting, the time had come, he decided, to take the first step toward having.

Maddy Dalton wanted him. That knowledge had settled sweetly in his conscious mind this afternoon and had heated his blood as well as his loins. It didn't take much effort to call to mind the image of her wet t-shirt clinging to her breasts and the way her nipples had beaded when he'd looked at them.

As he dried off and reached for a pair of loose fitting shorts, the rest of the afternoon's images flooded his thoughts, and Chase reveled in them. He had purposefully preened out there, and had been rewarded with not only Maddy's rapt attention, but Lucas's, too.

One look at the front of the older man's pants this afternoon as he'd stared at Chase's pecs had shown him which move he had to make first.

Lucas wanted him—and he didn't think the older man even realized the attraction was entirely mutual.

* * * *

Lucas toweled off after his shower, and in deference to the heat pulled on a clean pair of jeans but left his shirt off. Padding bare-foot into his kitchen, he opened the fridge and surveyed the contents. Most evenings he took his dinner in the bunkhouse with the rest of the crew. But sometimes, especially in the summer months, he preferred to just grab a sandwich and a beer on his own.

He'd been living in the foreman's house—a three bedroom single storey structure—since he'd become foreman of the Circle D nearly twenty years before. As a matter of fact, he hadn't been in residence long when Vic Reynolds hired on. It had been no problem making room for the man and his engaging son.

Lucas pulled a beer out of the fridge, opened it, and held the chilled bottle to his forehead.

Closing his eyes, he felt everything crashing in on him. He remembered the first time he set eyes on Chase Reynolds. It seemed like only yesterday. Images of the child he'd been, hungry to belong, intertwined with newer, more recent images. Over top of everything he recalled the emotions that had swirled within him just this afternoon. Emotions he had no business feeling. Lord help him, he'd looked at Chase's naked chest and been turned on as hotly as when he'd looked at Maddy's wet-cotton covered breasts.

At that moment, Lucas hated himself.

Down deep within his soul hid a secret he'd never shared with anyone, a secret he'd only acknowledged to himself alone and in the deep dark of night. But it lay at the heart of his being, the reason why at forty-one he remained a bachelor and would likely die one—a lonely old man with no one to call his own. This secret formed a ten-mile high wall between him and the emotions, the very real feelings he had for Maddy.

The knock on his front door drew him out of his reverie. He stepped out of the kitchen and into the parlor where he could easily see who had come calling.

"Mind if I come in?" Chase asked through the screen door.

"Not at all. You don't have to knock."

"Sure I do. In case you hadn't noticed, I'm not a kid anymore."

Lucas chose not to respond to that as the younger man came inside.

Pointing to the beer in Lucas's hand Chase asked, "Do you have an extra one of those?"

Lucas nodded, spun on his heel and headed back to the fridge. His heart pounded heavily in his chest. The sound of Chase's steps seemed to echo loudly in his ears and he knew the younger man followed him. It was fucking surreal to have Chase right here with him, to be alone with him considering the thoughts that had been swirling though his head in the last few moments.

Inhaling deeply, Lucas dug deep for his composure. Knowing that commodity to be shaky at best, and knowing he had no time or space to shore it up didn't fill him with confidence. But he couldn't tell the kid—the man—to go away and leave him alone. He couldn't, and he wouldn't. He'd just have to tough it out somehow.

Hadn't he been toughing it out, more or less hiding from reality, all of his adult life?

"Here, it's nice and cold," Lucas said as he turned, ready to extend his arm to hand the bottle to Chase. The younger man had stepped closer than he realized, and Lucas found his gaze captivated.

"Thanks. I wonder when the hell this heat wave is going to end." Chase took a long sip of beer, then released Lucas's gaze and stepped back.

Lucas didn't know whether to be relieved or not. He looked around the room then used his own bottle as a pointer, gesturing toward one of the chairs by the table, inviting his visitor to sit.

Chase took a seat, but Lucas felt too restless to settle anywhere. Instead, he remained standing with his back against the small counter. Maybe five feet separated them, and Lucas wondered if it would be enough distance to banish the images that had been playing peek-a-boo with his conscious thoughts all afternoon.

"The heat's been a real bitch," Lucas finally said, his brain scrambling to join the conversation. Unfortunately, talking about the afternoon's work—which brought back the *real* heat of the afternoon—wasn't helping in his quest. He needed to derail the conversation, redirect it. "Maddy insists on doing most the fence work herself. It always seemed to be the one chore no one else wanted to tackle on the place." And maybe Lucas needed to change the work schedule and not have him and Chase working together so closely. If he wanted to resist temptation, then the most logical thing for him to do would be to make sure he didn't get too close to either Chase or Maddy. *And isn't that a hell of a dilemma?* "But we're nearly done, now. Likely just another day on the fence line at most."

"Do you mind if I ask you a personal question?" Chase's tone sounded intimate to Lucas' ear—but that was probably just in his head. *I have to stop imagining things.*

Lucas' heart picked up speed. He had to swallow and lock down his imagination before he could speak. "Go ahead and ask."

"Why haven't you and Maddy gotten together? I can see you're attracted to each other. But I can also tell there's been no intimacy between you. Why not?"

If it had been anyone else asking that question, Lucas would have told them to mind their own damn business. But this was Chase, and the words warning him off just wouldn't come. He didn't know if he could give the younger man a completely truthful answer. Any scenario of that brought images of having his lights punched out. So he settled for a truthful, if ambiguous response. "It's complicated."

Silence coated the kitchen and Lucas was held motionless by the look in Chase's eyes. As penetrating a stare as any he'd ever received, it left him feeling completely naked.

His cock began to harden, and the bottom dropped out of his stomach when Chase flicked his gaze down to it.

"I thought so. Kind of hard to swing in one direction when you feel a pull in another at the same time, isn't it? But what you don't seem to understand, Lucas, is that you really don't have to choose. You *can* have it both ways."

"I don't think I follow you." He said the words, had to say them, because they were the only words he could say, the only words that made any sense. But deep inside he felt a dawning awareness, a seedling of knowledge that had just taken root. How could Chase have seen into his soul? How could he *know*? He couldn't know. He couldn't understand this terrible tug-of-war raging inside him. Unless...

"Lucas."

He'd never heard his name spoken in quite that way before. Drawn, he met Chase's gaze. The expression in those clear blue eyes arrowed straight to his gut, straight to that secret desire hiding within him. He couldn't stop the strangled sob that broke free from those depths. Desire, having lived in darkness all its life, had suddenly seen a ray of light and fairly screamed to be released.

Unable to face the younger man a moment longer, Lucas turned around. Both hands gripped the bottle of beer hard as, head bowed, his entire body shook with emotion.

A lifetime of living a lie, of pretense and pain and loneliness had stacked up, year upon year, bearing down on his soul with a weight that had grown with each day passed. Even as he felt the quaking, he knew his soul, his conscience, could hold it in no longer.

"Shh." Chase had left the chair and stood beside him, so close Lucas could feel the heat of him, smell the soap he'd used earlier. The younger man's voice had become a crooning, a gentle sound without words as he gently pried the bottle from Lucas' hands.

All this Lucas felt in a heartbeat. And more.

The sensation of a hand, strong but gentle stroking his back was something foreign and intoxicating. Supple fingers played across his shoulders, down his spine, then up to gently comb through his hair. Pulling him so that he leaned into the solid male chest, Chase's touch felt *good*. Better than good.

"Chase."

"I'm here. It's all right, love. I'm right here and everything is going to be all right."

Lucas could only stand still and absorb the gentle caresses with his heart hammering and his breath hitching. Undecided what to do with his hands, he gripped the edge of the sink. As his blood heated, his cock hardened even more. A groan rumbled from deep in his belly, a groan that spoke of arousal and need, and emotions that spiraled in directions he'd never dared truly imagine.

Any doubt he might have harbored about what was happening here in his kitchen fled when Chase pressed his hips against him and for the first time in his life Lucas felt the unmistakable ridge of another man's cock pushing against him. The strength of it thrilled him. Arousal and excitement wove together. Lucas liked the sensations, a lot.

"Do you want me to stop?" Chase whispered the question, his breath tickling Lucas' ear.

Did he want him to stop? Lucas had never planned to act on his attraction to Chase, just as he'd never acted on any of the attractions he'd felt toward other men over the years. He'd convinced himself that these feelings were an aberration; that they weren't real and could never be reciprocated, ever, by anyone.

He'd convinced himself that he was broken inside—flawed, *bad*. He'd believed the feelings inside him, the needs and desires to be one-sided and imaginary.

When Chase had come home a few days ago, Lucas thought his heart would burst, he felt so happy to see him. On the heels of that joy came an attraction, an infatuation that had first shocked and then shamed him.

It had never occurred to him that Chase could feel the same way.

Did he want him to stop?

"*No.* Don't stop. Please…but I…I don't know how…" He couldn't finish the thought because at that moment Chase reached down with his right hand and stroked Lucas' denim covered erection.

"Then I won't stop. And don't worry, I'll show you how. Do you still have that lock on your bedroom door?"

"I…yes." Lucas pressed his cock against the pressure of Chase's hand. He nearly laughed because he thought he reacted to the petting in the same way a love-starved puppy reacted to a gentle hand and a kind word.

"Come on. Let's go to where we can be assured of privacy. Last thing we need is someone knocking on the door and spoiling the mood."

Lucas was a novice being led by a wiser, more experienced man. That thought penetrated when Chase paused in the parlor and shut the inside front door and locked it. "No interruptions."

Lucas followed him down the short hall, so many emotions bubbling to the surface he became giddy with them, because the chief sensation was freedom.

He heard the bedroom door click closed behind them, heard the lock engage. Before he could turn around, Chase's arms came around him from behind, the embrace warm and strong. And then, whisper light, firm moist lips brushed against Lucas' neck and shoulder.

Lucas turned around then, the need in him so fierce it could no longer be contained. In Chase's eyes Lucas read desire and appreciation. Such kindness stared back at him he reacted instinctively. Leaning forward, Lucas tested the feel of Chase's lips against his own. One touch, and then another. Then gently, a kiss that was full, questing, a tasting and a statement all rolled into one. Chase's lips melded to his as his arms drew him closer. The touch of his tongue electrified Lucas. Starving, he opened his mouth and gave him full access.

Lucas reached for the front of his pants only to find Chase's hands already there. Eager, shaking, he swore softly when the garment hit the floor and Chase dropped to his knees and took Lucas' cock into his mouth.

Lucas's hands caressed the younger man's head, his fingers combing through his hair even as he shivered with pleasure.

Chase released him with a wet plop, his eyes focused as he looked up and asked, "Want to return the favor?"

Though he never had, Lucas nodded his head eagerly. Chase got to his feet and peeled off his own shorts and t-shirt. Kicking free of his pants, Lucas sprawled on the bed, pulling the younger man down with him.

Finally free to indulge what had always drawn him, Lucas encircled Chase's cock with his hand, the caress the same as he'd used on his own a hundred times before. But this caress thrilled him beyond measure. How arousing to hear Chase groan in response, to know he pleasured this hot young stud.

Leaning forward, he placed wet, open mouthed kisses on Chase's chest and belly, stroked muscled thighs with his hands as he worked his way down.

Pleasure became a quiver that flowed over his body as he took the hot, hard flesh into his mouth. The salty flavor, the delicate heat satisfied a craving he'd never admitted to himself he had. With lips and tongue, Lucas lavished attention on Chase, humbled and aroused when Chase shook and groaned in return. Then everything inside him rejoiced as he once more felt the hot moist caress of Chase's mouth on him.

The overwhelming urge to thrust, to take and claim and *own* transcended everything else, and as he moved his hips to meet the wet wild suction on his cock he rode the same motion from Chase. This joining of two into one felt more powerful, more basic than any he'd ever experienced before. This was a perfect mating of souls.

Rapture exploded, sharper, bolder, longer and Lucas swallowed even as he felt his own seed drawn from his body into Chase's eager mouth. Hot and heady, wild and wanton, the orgasm went on and on, each streaming pulse more potent than the one before until finally the last spasm faded. Still, Lucas was reluctant to release Chase, dotting tender kisses low on his belly.

"That was better than I had dreamed it would be," Chase whispered, and Lucas practically preened under the gentle petting Chase gave him.

"I never even dared to dream," Lucas admitted quietly.

"Have you had dinner?" Chase asked, stretching then bracing himself on his elbow.

Lucas turned on his side so he could see the other man's face. "This didn't count?"

Chase laughed, the sound fresh and young and uplifting. Lucas smiled. He wondered if the lightness of spirit he felt inside him could be seen on his face.

"Well, there *are* calories involved, but no. How about if we go make something for dinner? Then we can talk."

"I want more," Lucas said, his resolve firm. He'd crossed the barrier he'd lived behind all his life. There would be no going back. He wanted to experience everything he'd denied himself. At this moment on a Thursday night, he wanted it all.

"So do I. Let's eat first."

Lucas got to his feet and headed to his closet. Inside, a scant collection of clothes that he would wear on a Sunday, or to some social function or other laid limply on hangers. Also stored there, rarely used, hung two robes, both of them Christmas gifts from years past—one from Maddy, and one from a woman he'd dated for a time nearly a decade before.

He took the blue one down and extended it to Chase, then snagged the brown one for himself.

"I don't think I have a whole hell of a lot in my fridge," he said by way of apology as he belted the robe.

"As I recall, you never had a whole hell of a lot in that fridge."

"As *I* recall, you ate everything in sight, which was why it was usually empty."

Chase opened the bedroom door and turned to face him. Laughter lit his eyes and curved his mouth, and Lucas felt suddenly awed by the reality of what had just passed between them. Years may have separated them, but in that moment it seemed as if they'd never been apart.

Chase must have understood the expression on his face. Reaching out, he laid his hand on Lucas's shoulder.

"We have a lot to talk about."

"Yeah, we do."

Chapter 3

The stallion stood fierce and proud, descended from excellent bloodlines. His name was Knight Shadow, one of the K-Temple Ranch's stars, and worth more money than Maddy wanted to think about. Stud fees, though not as expensive for quarter horses as they could be for some race horses, cost dearly. But the Circle D had three beautiful mares also descended from excellent stock, and Maddy had cut a deal with Beth and Michael Templeton. In exchange for the conjugal visits about to take place, they would get their pick of the three foals.

Knight Shadow had arrived, on loan until all three mares had been serviced. One of the ladies, Francesca, was ready to go. Maddy fully expected the other two mares to become estrous within the next few days.

Maddy watched as Chase approach. He leaned on the railing of the corral beside her and together they observed the stallion prance around the outdoor paddock. He sniffed the air and announced his presence, accustoming himself to the new space and, Maddy thought, proclaiming his superiority.

"Ralph Meade is getting settled in the bunk house. Seems like a nice guy. That stallion, on the other hand, is magnificent. I'm not surprised the Templetons sent someone to guard their asset."

Maddy chuckled. "Every once in a while you say something that makes you sound as if you have a degree in business."

Chase's smile flashed, sending an immediate jolt to her belly. She'd done her best to put carnal thoughts of the younger man out of her mind since she'd seen him shirtless the other day. In this case, her best really wasn't good enough. She focused like a laser on their conversation.

"Well I can't really help that," Chase said. "I *do* have a degree in business. But I learned how to work right here, and this is home. So, when is the live sex show?"

Maddy thought she was going to choke. Chase patted her on the back until she could breathe again. She hadn't realized how much laughter her life had lacked until Chase came home.

"Just as soon as the cocktails and hors d'oeuvres are ready to serve the voyeurs."

It pleased her she could make him laugh in return.

"Seriously, I only every watched one mating session, and it had a decidedly…feral effect on me."

Oh, she really didn't think talking about sex in *any* context was a good idea. Maybe teasing would help. "If I recall, you were around fifteen at the time. For a fifteen-year-old boy, everything has a decidedly feral effect."

"You had a feral effect on me back then, and that certainly hasn't changed."

He turned his head to stare at her square on and the look he sent her settled right between her thighs.

Licking lips suddenly gone dry Maddy searched for a clever or even not-so-clever throwaway line. What she said wasn't what she'd meant to say. It came from deep down, a secret thought, a secret idea that had begun on an afternoon's work detail and ended that same evening as she'd seen the lights turned out in her foreman's house.

"Funny, I watched you go into Lucas' house the other night, and emerge the next morning and for some reason I figured *my* affect on you *had* changed."

"I've simply broadened my horizons, sweetheart, not changed them." He focused his attention for one moment on her breasts. His gaze met hers and she wondered she didn't burst into flames on the spot with the heat that look contained. In the next moment, Chase straightened up and took one step away from the fence.

"I promised Bill I'd give him a hand getting Francesca ready. Guess I'll see you over at the foaling barn later?"

"Yeah, later."

It was the best response Maddy could produce. Her mind suddenly filled with images more *feral* than the horses they'd been talking about. She wished she had time to sit and think about everything that had just happened between her and Chase. She hadn't missed that reference to his having come home, and that pleased her because that's how she felt about his return, too.

But all the other stuff had her heart pounding and her nipples tingling and she wanted to sit and think about them.

Unfortunately spare time was something she had in short supply at the moment. She needed to call the Templetons and let them know their man and their horse had arrived safe and sound. She also needed to send off an order to the supply store in Gunnison so they could get it together for pickup tomorrow. There was the fence-line to finish— and after the other day she wondered if she should just do that on her own—she had the breeding session to attend, and she needed to finish going over the ranch's financials. She only had so many fingers to keep on all the buttons. At times running the ranch could run *her* a bit ragged. As she walked, she shrugged her shoulders, dislodging tension and recent thoughts.

She'd been working on coming up with a five year plan for the ranch. As she headed toward the house, she wondered if maybe Chase would have some insights into that.

She'd never consulted anyone before on that level of ranch business. In the last few years, not even her father had been privy to all the details of the operation. She'd allowed him to think they just scraped by, because he'd taken a liking to the shopping channel, and while she hated to deny him anything, he'd damn near bankrupted her with his purchases. No, scratch the idea of having Chase give his read on things. When you let other people get that close, they just screwed everything up on you, leaving you with a bigger mess and more work than you had to begin with.

At least that had always been her experience.

* * * *

Chase felt positively Machiavellian.

He'd kept his eye out for Maddy, knowing that she would insist on being present for the breeding. From what he'd seen in the short week he'd been home, Maddy pretty much insisted on being everywhere and doing everything. As he'd focused on the owner of the Circle D it hadn't taken him long to understand two very important things: first, Maddy had control issues. Very serious and very deep-seated control and trust issues; second, coping-wise, she was hanging on by a thread.

Chase figured she needed to relax and unwind, and knew that had to happen very soon. The other part of his prescription—the control and trust issues—would take longer to deal with.

Chase hoped that over time, he and Lucas could help her with that control problem. He didn't expect over-night results there, because trust took time to build. But he knew one surefire cure for the stress she seemed to be suffering from, and that cure would be immediate.

He remembered the raw physicality of horses mating and wondered what sort of an effect that would have on her in her current frame of mind. He'd also deliberately teased her earlier, deliberately put images of sex front and center in her thoughts, and knew all that would be in play as the horse handlers—and the stallion—did their jobs.

When Maddy entered the foaling barn, she went straight over to Bill, who had Francesca on a short rein, soothing her. Not too many people were allowed in the area—a moderate-sized indoor paddock— at this juncture. Francesca would be nervous enough. Bill was preparing to cover her eyes as horses had a very fine fight or flight instinct. Plus, you never knew how a mare would react during mating.

"This will be her first time. I think she knows what's coming, and she's a bit afraid." Lucas' voice washed over him. Chase met his eyes and couldn't hold back the smile which he knew to be intimate, because that's how it felt. Lucas continued his observation.

"I can really sympathize with her."

Chase wanted to hug Lucas, but didn't dare. Someday, when the other man felt more comfortable with their relationship, a public display of affection might be possible. But for now, since Chase couldn't hug him, he used the tone of his voice to soothe him.

"I told you there was no rush on that. I'm perfectly happy just having oral sex with you. We've got all the time in the world."

"I appreciate that. But I want more, even if the prospect has me nervous."

Chase watched Lucas's eyes track over to Maddy, and noticed the softening of his expression. When he realized Chase had noticed, he flushed.

"Sorry."

"Don't be sorry. We're both of the same mind there. I'm looking forward to our first time together."

Lucas nodded, his eyes on Maddy as she listened to Bill. When she walked toward the door and took up her position along the wall, he looked back at Chase.

"How are we going to manage that, exactly?"

Chase smiled. He wouldn't tell Lucas that he'd done what he could to manipulate the situation already. Later, he'd be completely open and honest with both his lovers. But not quite yet. For now he could tell him part of it, all true.

"We'll watch and take our chance when we see it."

"You think she'll be receptive? To having both of us? At the same time?"

"I do." *Interesting words.* In Chase's mind, he was building a serious relationship with Lucas. He wanted one with Maddy, too.

The large door at the other side of the room opened, and Ralph Meade, the horse handler from K-Temple Ranch, entered leading Knight Shadow.

The stallion stopped once he got inside the indoor paddock, his head raising as he sniffed the air. Giving a fierce scream, he managed to lift up on his two hind legs before Meade could control him.

The scent of his mate in the air, his cry one of dominion, staking his claim.

Francesca, even with her eyes covered, sensed the moment. Her flesh quivered, as if she'd been overtaken by a premonition so primal it took her back to truly feral times.

Chase turned his attention on Maddy, who just at that moment turned hers gaze on him. Enough space separated them to protect her personal space, but not so much that she couldn't see his face, read the intent in his gaze, and he held nothing back.

She licked her lips and jerked her attention back to the horses, just as Ralph led the stallion forward.

Chase had helped Bill put cloth around Francesca's hind legs and hooves, because while often times the process of mating happened with relative calm, the mare docile and receptive, sometimes the lady did kick up a fuss. Since you never knew how the session would play out, it was best to do what you could to protect both horses from harm.

Chase had once read that in the wild sometimes the mating between mare and stallion could be fierce, bordering on the violent. Certainly the one other time he'd mentioned to Maddy had been just such an event.

Shadow screamed again, and Chase noted that all eyes had turned to the horse. The animal obviously understood his role. Chase knew the scent of the mare had caused a distinct physical reaction in him, and everyone in the barn could clearly see he was ready to go.

There existed tools handlers sometimes had to employ to assist the stallion in his work—if he somehow wasn't sufficiently motivated—but Chase didn't think Shadow would need any assistance from humans to get the job done today.

Bill and Charlie stood at Francesca's head. As the stallion approached, the mare shifted nervously, bobbing her head up and down as if trying to reason with her handlers. When Shadow nuzzled her back, she kicked out, her neigh easily interpreted by all present—horse or human, the feminine cry of distress sounded nearly the same.

Chase cut his glance over to find Maddy staring at him. Even as the sound of the stallion once more announcing his claim echoed off the walls, Chase felt his one eyebrow rise and didn't need a mirror to know an expression of masculine superiority had overtaken his features. While she watched, he repositioned himself so that Lucas stood between them. Subtly, he smoothed one hand down the other man's back, played it across his ass.

No one but Maddy saw gesture, and it pleased Chase enormously that she understood it and reacted to it. Even with the distance between them, Chase could see her nipples pucker against her shirt, and caught the slight sway of her hips—as if she'd clamped her legs together in an instinctive reaction to arousal.

"I've never seen Maddy look like that before," Lucas whispered. "Is she all right?"

Lucas had admitted to him the night before that he wasn't very good at reading people. Chase figured that, over time, he'd improve.

"She's fine."

Shadow would no longer be denied. He mounted the fractious mare, giving her a gentle nip when she protested and tried to shake off both him and her handlers. The moment he penetrated her, she whinnied sharply, shivered, and then calmed. Though she labored for breath, she no longer fought off the mating. Bill and Charlie had to work at holding her still, however, because of the strength of the stallion thrusting into her.

The entire process didn't take longer than a few minutes. Shadow dismounted when he was finished, no longer interested in the mare now that nature had prevailed.

"Too many pheromones in the air," Lucas said.

Chase looked down, took in the ridge of the erection tenting Lucas' jeans. Bill and Charlie had all their attention taken up soothing Francesca, Ralph had already turned, leading Shadow away. The only one who looked their way was Maddy.

Chase reached down and stroked Lucas's erection through the denim of his jeans.

Lucas leaned into the caress then turned to him. "Let's break free of this crowd for a half hour." The pleading tone told Chase exactly how he wanted to spend that half hour. Chase suddenly smiled.

"Maddy?" Bill's call was to a retreating female back.

Chase had been watching her, and had recognized the look on her face just before she turned and practically fled the building. What he'd seen had been raw lust.

"She mentioned earlier she wasn't feeling well," Chase lied, his comments directed to the other two men. "You guys go ahead and finish up. Lucas and I will check on Maddy."

"Someone in Marshville mentioned some sort of bug making the rounds," Bill announced, concerned. "I'll get some chicken soup started as soon as I'm done here. Maybe you guys can take some up to her later, if she's feeling poorly."

"Good idea," Chase agreed.

"Maddy didn't say she felt ill, did she?" Lucas asked as they left the barn and headed toward the main house.

"No, she didn't, and she doesn't."

"Then why are we checking on her?"

"We're not so much checking on her as we are seizing an opportunity."

Chase saw the exact instant that Lucas understood his meaning. "Do you really think she's ready for us?"

"I think she's at least ready to talk. So let's go see how she's doing, and take it from there?"

"You really believe that she'll be interested in a relationship with both of us at the same time."

Did he? Not every woman would be interested in taking on two men who also would take on each other. But he'd tested the waters already and knew part of what had gotten Maddy so hot, so fast, had been watching his attention to Lucas. So to his lover, he said, "Oh yeah. I think if we handle it just right she'll want us both."

* * * *

Maddy was shaking inside by the time she reached the house. Taking only a moment to kick off her boots, she practically ran to her bedroom.

Nothing like this had ever happened to her before. She'd been slightly aroused, thanks to Chase's sly innuendos and blatant flirting. She'd watched him stroke Lucas, and that man had nearly melted under his touch. Then as the horses had performed, she'd looked over, caught sight of Chase and Lucas, both aroused. Chase had reached toward Lucas and suddenly her imagination had flashed a full color three dimensional freeze frame image of the three of them—Lucas, Chase, and herself—totally naked and fully engaged in hot, raunchy sex.

She'd nearly had an orgasm on the spot.

But she hadn't, had in fact been left hot and high and at the very edge so that the only thing she could think, the only thing she could do, was squirrel herself away and do something about it, *right now*.

She honestly believed if she didn't have an orgasm in the next few minutes she would incinerate from the heat running through her body.

Once inside her room she whipped off her tee-shirt and shucked her bra and jeans. Falling onto the bed, she didn't even take time to remove her panties, only pushed them down and out of the way. Then her hand found her sex, lightly stroking back and forth, seeking out her clit. The friction seared, tiny shivers of arousal shooting sparks to every part of her. For one fleeting second she wished she'd gone to her dresser first to get her vibrator. But she didn't want to stop long enough to get it now. She couldn't stop. Her hand kept stroking, her fingers dipping slightly into the moisture that had already gathered. She burned so hot it nearly drove her insane. Closing her eyes, she tried to focus on the image that had hurled her to this point of frantic need. She never would have thought the idea of two men being intimate together would turn her on, but it had. Maybe it wasn't the idea of just any two men, but two who somehow, despite everything, she considered to be *hers*. And that vision of the three of them together… What would it be like? How would it feel? It had been so long since she'd had sex, she could barely recall the sensation of a man's cock pushing into her. What would it be like to have sex with two men at the same time?

Her climax eluded her and she whimpered, frustration mounting by the second. Bearing down with every ounce of will she possessed, keeping her eyelids closed even more tightly, she focused on the images that had catapulted her to this, tried to imagine how it would feel to have two lovers petting her, arousing her, *servicing* her at the same time.

As her hand brushed frantically against her feminine flesh, it was joined by another, masculine one. And then another.

Maddy gasped, opening her eyes wide. Chase stretched out on her right, Lucas on her left. Both men had a hand each on her pussy, their touch both strange and familiar at the same time. She froze, a cry trapped in her throat. The heat of embarrassment flooded her face.

"Hush, honey. We're here now. We'll take care of you. We'll all take care of each other." Chase's outrageous pronouncement was accompanied by that devil grin, and the sensation of his finger penetrating her.

"Maddy."

She turned instinctively to Lucas. Her name had been a whispered plea that brushed her face, his voice hoarse with need. His lips came down on hers, his tongue bold, the kiss totally carnal. One of his hands caressed the top of her head while the other settled more firmly between her thighs. Then, he mimicked Chase and plunged one of his fingers deep inside her.

Chapter 4

"Let go, sweetheart." Chase whispered in her right ear while Lucas's tongue continued doing amazing things to her mouth.

Action followed his words—he took her hand off her pussy, and stretched her arm above her head.

"Seeing this brass headboard is giving me all sorts of ideas. Ever been tied up before?"

"Never," Maddy panted as she tilted her hips up, and spread her legs. Lucas had weaned his lips from hers, only to begin placing kisses and licks on her chin and neck.

The sound of masculine laughter vibrated wetly against her flesh. "We'll have to add that to our list of things to try," Lucas said.

"You're hot, baby. You are so incredibly hot for us."

Chase's praise was so welcome she didn't even mind when Lucas took her left hand and placed it with the right. She felt stretched out, and though there wasn't a restraint in sight, she could imagine her wrists bound to the bed. She could imagine being staked out, naked, a feast waiting to be consumed by these two virile men. Imagination, fueled by arousal, yearned for reality.

"I've imagined you here like this for so long. Imagined having you naked, under my hands." Lucas' words fired her blood. He bent his head down and captured her left nipple in his mouth. It felt so good, she arched, a silent offering. He suckled strongly and Maddy whimpered, the sensation so amazing, she needed more. She'd barely begun to imagine what it would be like to have two men stroking her body, feeding her fires. Already reality outstripped imagination.

Chase took that moment to nuzzle her cheek. Unable to resist, she turned her head toward him and sought his mouth, losing herself in his kiss. Hot, hungry, he fairly devoured her. His tongue dominated her own, while his lips caressed and lavished hers. And all the while male fingers moved in and out of her hot, slick passage, and a hot, wet male mouth suckled her nipple.

"You're so wet and ready for us, baby. We both want to bury our cocks deep inside you, Maddy. Which one of us do you want inside you first? "

Chase's question only drove her higher. She had no control—not over her body, and not over her orgasm, which drew closer even as it skittered away. Words required too much effort, because everything inside her focused on her body and the delicious sensations flooding her. She didn't care whose cock fucked her first, as long as one of them did, and soon.

Chase seemed to sense her struggle. She saw him look over at Lucas, and in the next instant that man got off the bed. She turned her head and watched as he dropped his clothes to the floor.

He was gorgeous. How many times had she wondered what Lucas Calhoun looked like under his clothes? A man her age, over forty, he had not an ounce of flab on him. Muscled, tanned, his chest and arms rippled with power and strength. He made Maddy's mouth water. How many times had she thought about having him? Just the other day she'd imagined needing a few shots of whiskey to give her the courage to act on the attraction that had laid dormant between them all these years. Now, as he peeled his jeans and boxers off, her attention riveted on to his cock. Proud and erect, thick and long, she wondered what it tasted like. She didn't need whiskey now. She just needed him, needed to feel that hot hard rod push into her.

"Here, love. You'll need this."

She turned to look at Chase, still sprawled beside her. He'd taken his hand off her and reached into his jeans pocket, pulling out a handful of condoms. All but one he tossed on the bedside table. The one he kept, he opened.

Lucas knelt on the bed between Maddy's thighs. Captivated, she watched as Chase reached out, stroked Lucas' cock. Lucas closed his eyes, thrusting into that touch. Maddy imagined Chase was reluctant to let him go. But he did, and smoothed the protection into place.

Then Chase took hold of Lucas' rod once more and, gently pulling, brought him to her. Maddy's mind flashed to the image in the foaling barn, and suddenly she felt as if she was being handled, serviced. But rather than dampening her fires, the image damn near made her come on her own. Chase gave her his lover's cock, and the sight of his subtle dominance called to some inner instinct within her, one she'd never known she had inside her.

Nothing she had ever seen had fired Maddy's arousal so high as that.

"Our woman needs your cock right now more than I do. She needs you to fuck her. Don't you, Maddy?"

"Yes…please…*fuck me.*" She'd gone beyond caring about anything except having these two hot studs take her and pleasure her. She wanted nothing more than to please them too and come and come until no energy remained inside her.

The back of Chase's hand and the tip of Lucas' cock brushed her dewy folds at the same instant. And then Lucas entered her, his hard cock opening her lips, forcing them back as he pushed in, sank deeper and deeper inside her. She was tight because it had been so very long since she'd had a man's cock there. Shivering in ecstasy, Maddy savored every hot hard inch pushing in.

Lucas slid his arms around her, bringing her closer as his mouth took hers once more. Nearly frantic with need, Maddy wrapped arms and legs around him, her tongue tasting and claiming in the same hurried cadence of his thrusts within her.

He ended their kiss, levering the top of his body up and away from her for a moment. She felt a hand on the side of her face, turning her head.

Chase had stripped himself naked, his cock as beautiful, as hard and as ready as Lucas's. Instinct had her opening her mouth, stretching up so she could capture it with her lips.

Chase slid his dick into her mouth as surely and deeply as Lucas plumbed the depths of her pussy. He tasted exotic, as exotic as rapturous dreams in the middle of the night.

Where she and Lucas joined, the coarse hair surrounding his cock brushed and abraded her clit. The twin sensations, smooth and rough, the scents of Chase's hot penis and Lucas' perspiration all worked together to fling Maddy over the edge. Unable to stop herself, she opened her mouth, her cry of release nearly a scream.

On and on the waves of orgasm battered her, a climatic cyclone that held her fast, narrowed her consciousness so that the only thing she knew was her body, and those now a part of it.

Opening her eyes as the climax shivered down one level, she watched in awe and arousal as Lucas leaned forward and replaced her mouth on Chase's cock with his own.

Lucas began to come, thrusting in her hard and fast and deep. She felt the deep pulsing, even as she watched Chase's cock begin to spasm in Lucas's mouth.

Unexpected and fierce, Maddy's second orgasm shattered over her.

* * * *

Lucas ran his hand gently down Maddy's chest, the kind of lavish petting he'd yearned to give her for so long. Late afternoon shadows played out the window. He flicked his gaze over to her bedside clock.

Maddy lay between him and Chase. Her eyes were closed but he knew she wasn't sleeping. They had a lot to talk about, the three of them. And they needed time to do it.

"We left the others with the impression that you weren't feeling well," he said.

She didn't open her eyes but her smile reassured him, as did her words. "Funny. I feel great." Then her brow creased, and she opened her eyes. "If a bit confused."

"Thought I'd go over to the bunkhouse and collect some dinner for us. Reassure them you're fine, just in need of a rest."

"That's a good idea. We can eat together."

Chase's agreement stroked his emotions in the same way Maddy's gentle smile did. Embolden, he gave them the rest of his thoughts.

"I'm confused too, but not about how I feel right here, right now. So, since tomorrow is Sunday, I think we all should take the day off, relax, and try to figure things out." When Maddy looked at him, he simply returned her stare.

Generally, Sunday was a day off for everyone except Maddy. Lucas thought it past time she had a few days of R & R herself.

"Are you telling me what to do?"

Maddy's question came quietly, some might say almost casually. But Lucas knew her and knew better. "No, darlin', I'm making a suggestion."

"No one is going to take being boss of the Circle D away from you, sweetheart." Chase said. "But in the last couple of hours, we've begun something here, the three of us—mutually and consensually—something that's more than a just a one night stand. We're in this together. Let's see what we can make of it."

Lucas couldn't help but smile as Chase talked. The two of them occupied the same page, and had since their first time together a few days before. It was new and exciting and far and away more than Lucas had ever imagined he could ever have for himself. For the first time in his adult life he felt *good*, deep to the bottom of his soul good.

He and Chase had already formed a bond. Having Maddy join them, in his mind, would make everything complete. But there were hurdles they needed to surmount, and he knew it. He let his gaze roam Chase's body. All three of them had hurdles to jump, for although among them Chase seemed the more sexually self-assured, he had baggage, too. Lucas didn't know what, but he sensed its presence.

"All right. I need a shower. And I'd like to take it alone."

Lucas bent down and placed a kiss, lightly, on her lips. She would try and withdraw and find her defenses, he knew. And that was fine with him.

Apparently Chase agreed. "While you shower, Lucas will go speak to the men and get our dinner, and I'll go grab us both some clothes and set the table."

Because he watched her and knew her probably better than she thought he did, Lucas said, "We'll want to shower too, and put on fresh clothes before we eat."

"Of course. This is…this is just different."

"There are no hard and fast rules, sweetheart. We can make up our own as we go along," Lucas said, repeating Chase's words to him from just the night before. He'd thought about what he and the younger man had discussed late into the night, and just about everything Chase had said made perfect sense.

The normal rules of society and relationships didn't apply to them. He wondered what they could come up with, together, even as he worried that whatever they built together might not last.

* * * *

"Don't you worry about a damn thing. I told you I'd get my hands on that ranch, and I will. I just need a little more time."

"More time? You were *supposed* to have persuaded that bitch by now. You told me you'd have the property ready to sell to us by June first. Instead, I find out you've pissed her off to the point she won't even speak to you. You only have a couple of weeks left. Do I have to remind you that you've already been given a considerable down payment?"

Kevin Marsh cruised the back roads between Marshville and the Circle D ranch, his pace a meandering one. Timing was everything. He wanted to arrive at Maddy's after she'd had a chance to shower, have her dinner. Nothing turned him off more than the smell of cow shit. He didn't know why Maddy insisted on playing cow girl, but he'd soon put an end to that.

Marsh blamed the unexpected heat of the mid-May day for the sweat forming on his brow. He wouldn't allow himself to believe for even one moment that his discomfort had anything to do with his current conversation. Barnes might have a ton of money, but he, Marsh, was the leading citizen in his part of the county. *Time to put the New York upstart in his place.*

"Now you look here, Barnes. Things work differently out here in Colorado than they do in New York City. Old man Dalton's barely cold in the ground. It wouldn't have been seemly for Maddy to get married too soon. I pushed when I shouldn't have, is all. She's a woman, she'll get over it. Doesn't hurt to let her think she's calling the shots for a bit. But the time's about right, and I'm going to be making my move in the next day or so." And when he did, once he had her right where he wanted her, he'd teach her a thing or two about a woman's proper place. "I'll have the property ready to transfer into your name way before your construction start date of July tenth. So back off and let me work my magic."

"From what I've seen so far, you've got no magic."

"Maddy Dalton isn't like the bimbos you're used to, Barnes. Truth is I've got several aces up my sleeve where she's concerned." And one of them looked to be extremely promising. He didn't have everything he needed in his hands right at this moment, but he would after tonight. He smiled as he decided to give her a few hints right away. Besides, she should be damn grateful for the opportunity he was about to hand her.

Maddy had already reached the ripe old age of forty, and with no prospects in sight what-so-ever. He knew everyone hereabouts, and aside from some rough and tumble ranch hands there were no men available for Maddy to hook up with besides him. Many considered him the most eligible bachelor around, and plenty of women would do whatever he asked for a chance to be his wife. But he'd set his sights on Maddy, for obvious reasons.

He didn't think she knew he owned a good-sized piece of property on her eastern border. He needed her ranch because of the stream and the hot spring it had, and because of the combined size when added to his. Barnes and his cartel offered to pay huge for this piece of Colorado. He stood to make money twice, too—first, by selling the land outright; and second, by the increase of tourist flow through Marshville. As owner of two of the major businesses in Marshville, he'd be raking in the profits hand over fist.

Barnes had already advanced him a quarter of a million dollars on the deal, based on his word and the property he already owned. Being a smart businessman, Kevin had immediately invested that money in other projects, projects that would take time to pay off. Of course he'd also bought himself a few amenities. This brand new Caddy really represented a business investment, too. It shouted success, which meant anyone wanting to buy or sell real estate for miles around would see him as the most successful man for the job.

"Our agreement didn't mention the construction start date, but June first. I'm going to hold you to that, Marsh."

"Keep your damn pants on, Barnes. I'll have everything well in hand in the next couple of days."

Marsh didn't give the man an opportunity to bitch any further. He hung up and tossed the cell phone onto the seat beside him.

They way he saw it he'd been more than patient with Maddy. Things would already be settled if old man Dalton had waited just a couple more weeks to kick off. He'd had an agreement drawn up, giving him power of attorney for Dalton's estate. He knew he wouldn't have had any trouble getting that ornery old coot to sign it, either. The old bastard had been a real hard ass when it had come to his daughter. Maddy would have found herself in a position where she'd have had to marry him if she wanted to stay on her precious ranch. Robert Dalton's untimely demise had put paid to that plan, so he'd tried to court Maddy good and proper, stressing that her daddy would be smiling down from heaven if she did what any self-respecting woman without any other prospects for matrimony would do. But had she listened? All right, maybe he had gotten pissed off and tried to get some of his own back by giving the bitch a hard time lately. So he'd cast about for other options to get her where he needed her. Gone fishing is what he'd done. He hadn't been dishing B. S. to Barnes about having the situation under control soon.

He did have a couple irons in the fire where Maddy Dalton was concerned, and the time had come for him to test at least one of them.

Chapter 5

Chase didn't waste any time gathering things from his area of the bunkhouse and Lucas' place. Maddy was still in the shower when he returned. Not wanting to push her too far, too fast, he dumped their clothes in the bedroom that used to belong to Mr. Dalton.

It felt weird standing in that room, and not seeing the old man propped up in his wingback chair, ready to play a game of checkers. When Chase had first met the gruff owner of the Circle D, he'd been a boy of ten, newly suffering the loss of his mother and having been wrenched away from everything familiar and dumped into the hands of a father he couldn't remember.

Mr. Dalton had been partially incapacitated by then and wasted no time letting him know they had one thing had in common—having life crap on them. He would forever regret that he hadn't returned here, sooner. He'd never thanked Robert Dalton properly for his kindnesses, and he wished he had.

Putting more somber thought aside, Chase headed to the kitchen, making quick work of setting the table. He supposed to a certain extent he considered himself in control of this situation. He had a definite agenda that included Maddy and Lucas, true. But his manipulation of the situation, and them certainly wasn't malicious. He cared for them both a great deal, and would never do anything to deliberately hurt either one of them.

He looked up, a sixth sense alerting him. Maddy stood at the door to the kitchen. He'd never seen her look so unsure of herself, and he knew that wasn't what she'd intended at all. She'd wanted to shower alone in order to have the chance to put her defenses back in place, reconstruct the walls he and Lucas had already battered. But despite her outward appearance, her words to him had a bite.

"You seem to be making yourself right at home."

God, she's got spirit. I love that. He couldn't stop his huge grin. "Gee, Maddy, just a few days ago you urged me to do exactly that."

"You know what I mean."

"Sure I do, sweetheart. The question is, do you?"

When she just stared at him he went with his instincts, walked over to her, and gently pulled her into his arms. He said nothing, just rubbed her back gently and waited. Lucas came into the kitchen just then, carrying a tray piled high with burgers and fries—and one bowl of chicken soup.

"It's more than just sex, isn't it? I mean, I know you said it was more than a one-night stand, but it is more than sex. Isn't it?" Maddy asked the question against his chest, but he heard it clearly.

And so did Lucas.

"Of course it is. For all of us." Lucas' tone held that same note of tenderness that never ceased to stroke Chase's heart.

Chase put her back from him just far enough that he could see her face—and she could see his. "We've all got baggage, Maddy. And I don't think any of us has any idea exactly what this relationship of ours is, exactly. But yeah, it's a hell of a lot more than sex."

Her smile was fledgling, but there. She looked over at the tray of food Lucas still held.

"I'll put that to warm in the oven while you guys shower and change."

* * * *

"The reason I left when I did wasn't because Dad decided to pack it in. We *did* leave at the same time, but he'd made it clear he considered his obligations to me met the day I turned sixteen. He gave me a ride as far as Colorado Springs, made sure I had bus money. Then I was on my own."

"Son-of-a-bitch! Damn it to hell, Chase, you could have stayed here," Lucas exploded.

"Dad and I talked about helping you get into college," Maddy echoed Lucas, and Chase had to smile. "You really should have stayed."

"I couldn't. By then I had feelings for both of you and no idea in hell what to do about them."

Chase watched Maddy process that information. "So you've always been…" She stopped mid-sentence, her face turning a brilliant red.

"Bi-sexual?" Chase finished for her. When she nodded, he said, "Yes. Didn't understand it at first, but yes, I always have been. And I think I had to go away—just so I could come back."

"I think I always have been too, though I didn't ever put a label on myself," Lucas said quietly.

Dinner had been eaten, and they sat out on Maddy's front porch. He and Luc each held a bottle of beer, but Maddy had opted for coffee.

"I don't think that I could ever…I mean, I've never even *thought* about having sex with another woman." Maddy blushed again, shrugged, and looked as if she wanted to apologize for the size of the Christmas turkey.

"You don't have to, sweetheart, and I for one certainly don't expect it." Tricky, tricky ground, Chase thought. They all three tread very lightly. But at least they were treading.

"I'd say more than three would definitely be a crowd," Lucas added. "I can only tell you how I feel. For the first time ever, I'm with two people I trust, two people who know my deepest secret, and it's okay. Being *me* is okay, and I can't begin to tell you how liberating that feels. And if there has to be rules to whatever this is we have, then that should be one of them. We can all be ourselves, and it's okay."

The sound of a car coming down the long lane toward the house caught their attention. A band new, shiny Cadillac DTS carefully made its way toward them.

"Who drives the pimp-mobile?" Chase asked.

Maddy burst out laughing while Luc's chuckle came quieter. "That would be Kevin Marsh," he said.

The car pulled to a stop and a lone man emerged. Pudgy, he sported a white Stetson, white shirt with the sleeves rolled up, tan dress pants, and what looked to Chase like five hundred dollar boots. Something about the popinjay set his protective antenna to quivering and his back up.

"Evening, Maddy."

"Kevin."

"Thought I'd come out, see how you're doing."

"I'm fine."

Chase swallowed his laughter. Marsh didn't have any clue that he'd just been dismissed.

"Thought you might invite me in for a bit, so you and I can talk. Without the hired hands around."

Chase thought Marsh said the words 'hired hands' the same way someone else might utter the phrase 'rag pickers'.

"You should have called first, Kevin. As it is, I have plans." Maddy's tone emerged cool and laid back, but Chase could see she hated Marsh, and hated having to deal with him. He also noticed that she kept moving her gaze to both him and Lucas. Did she think either of them would deny her the right to fight her own battles, if that's what she wanted to do?

"If I had called, you'd have said for me not to come out." Marsh spread his hands, out, the chuckle jovial-sounding, as if he shared a joke with close friends. Looking closely at the man Chase could see the humor didn't reach his eyes. He was willing to admit that he might be prejudiced by what he'd already heard about this character, but Chase decided that didn't matter. He didn't like Kevin Marsh, not one little bit.

"Kevin, you're more insightful than I gave you credit for." Maddy sounded polite, but Chase could tell her manners were wearing thin.

"Why don't you two cow pokes go on back to the bunkhouse where you belong?" Marsh had addressed that to him and Lucas.

Though Chase felt tempted to hot-foot it down the porch steps and plant his fist in Marsh's face, he merely looked over at Maddy. Since she sat between himself and Lucas, he could see that man's expression and understood they both occupied the same page, both of them exercising enormous restraint.

"Well, now you see, Kevin, that's the problem. Those plans that I just mentioned I already have *involve* these two fine gentlemen. I have an idea! Why don't you go back to town where *you* belong?"

Chase had to admire Maddy's poise.

"Well, now, Maddy, there's no need to be like that. I thought you and I could at least be neighborly. You know, visit a spell and trade gossip. Why, just yesterday I ran into Doc Albertson over in Colorado Springs. I told him what a fine job he'd done taking care of your pa, especially those last five or six months when poor old Robert had to have been in so much pain. Told him if I ever got myself in a bad way, I'd want the same kind of super-duper pain relievers he prescribed for good old Robert. Funniest damn thing. He seemed to think he'd only prescribed mild Percocet for your dad."

"Is that a fact?"

Chase didn't know what had just happened, but the change in Maddy was palpable. An edge of tension covered her that hadn't been there just a moment before.

"That is a fact. Sure got me to wondering. You may not know it, but I can be like a bulldog when something gets me to wondering. Why, I just won't let it go until I have me an answer."

"Maybe you have too much time on your hands, Kevin. You need to get yourself a hobby, or something."

"I already have a hobby, and a new one at that. Mystery solving. Matter of fact, I'm headed over to Colorado Springs right now to meet a few people who might be able to help me with my latest mystery." Marsh's smile spread wide, but the look he sent to all three of them— Maddy included—seethed with malevolence.

"You best get going then, before you lose the light of the day. Be a shame if you got lost on the back country roads."

He didn't say another word, just tipped his hat in a way Chase could only describe as insulting. Chase remained silent as Marsh got into his car and drove off. Lucas didn't have as much patience.

"What the hell was that all about?"

Chase looked at Maddy, waiting for her to answer. On Luc's face he read confusion, and on Maddy's, prevarication.

"Just Kevin being a pain in the ass. Poking around to see if he can find any weakness, anyway to cause hurt or pain. Sort of like a fishing expedition, I expect. Like I said, just Kevin being a pain in the ass."

"He does it very well." Chase said

Maddy's answer left a lot to be desired. The fact that Lucas took it at face value and agreed with her stopped Chase from pressing the matter further.

He'd already figured out that one thing that drove Maddy—and likely the reason she hadn't let any man ever get close to her—was her fear of not being in control.

He could only hope she would eventually learn to surrender that commodity from time to time.

* * * *

The mesa called to her, flat and open and removed from the ranch and its challenges and joys. Her horse, a beautiful mare named

Diamond, pawed the ground anxiously, proving to Maddy that the need to run and be free wasn't only her own.

She looked over her shoulder, letting her eyes sweep over everything that belonged to her, everything that she had worked and sweated and fought for over the last nearly twenty years.

She had stayed after college because this was home, and her father had needed her. And she'd needed to take care of him, too.

As she watched, two men on horseback came into view. She didn't find it at all strange that she would recognize them, even from this distance. She knew they saw her, too. And she didn't know what to think when Lucas and Chase just stayed there, watching her. Letting her have her space.

Turning around, she put her heels to Diamond, urging the horse to race with the wind. Together they ate up ground, the lay of the land familiar to them both. Here the angle of ascent was discreet, a long upward sweep that took energy and time to climb. Here in any direction she cared to look the land belonged to her.

So what?

She slowed Diamond to a walk. They had reached the Mesa and as she turned the mare in a tight circle, taking in the vista that formed her birthright, the question echoed inside her again.

So what? There would be no children to pass this legacy on to. She'd decided she would never marry, because she didn't want the emotional demands of marriage. Children would be even more of an emotional drain, wouldn't they?

Besides, she didn't believe in marriage—oh the ideal of it sounded lovely as hell, but she'd never seen one that lasted more than a handful of years. Her father had been on her ass the last couple years of his life, haranguing her at every opportunity, demanding a son-in-law, and grandbabies, so he could die in peace.

She'd been willing to do almost anything for the man, despite his irascibility. But not that. God, the argument echoed in her memory, so familiar she could hear it even now. *"Ain't natural a woman your age not having a man to take care of her."* Oh yeah, she loved that one. He a man, she a woman, and who the hell had been taking care of whom for more years that she cared to admit? Her standard line had almost become her mantra. Marriage was nothing more than a vow that could be faked, a promise that could be broken and a piece of paper easily shredded.

She'd never yearned for that particular version of the American Dream. Those desires—for hearth and home, husband and children—had never been in her. Maybe that had been God's way of building her, so that when her years of caring for her father came to an end, she'd be free.

Free to do what?

Thoughts of her father brought back Kevin's visit the evening before. She shivered, a chill skittering along her flesh. He'd been threatening her; that much seemed clear. How much did Kevin Marsh know? Did his having that knowledge pose a threat to her? The man was a worm, and she honestly didn't know anyone who really liked him. If he only possessed the knowledge of what she'd done, it would be his word against hers. She felt pretty confident that she'd come out of that competition on top. But if he had some form of proof, then what?

She guided her horse down the slope, taking a trail that would lead to the stream and small stand of trees that grew there. The water helped keep the trees alive even in drought years, and the shade they provided allowed the grass to stay soft and supple through most of the summer.

When she'd been a child, she'd wanted to camp there, simply because it was one of the prettiest spots she'd ever seen. She'd not been allowed to, of course, not alone. Wild animals still roamed this part of Colorado. Maddy smiled. When she'd gotten older, the allure of those long ago fantasies had faded.

The older you got, the less you wanted to sleep on the hard, unforgiving ground.

Diamond whinnied, and Maddy directed her gaze ahead to see what had caught the attention of her horse. There, by the stand of trees, two horses stood, seeming alone. She recognized the mounts, of course. She imagined Chase and Lucas lazing about in the shade of the trees.

Last night, she'd felt certain one or the other of them would have tried to take over that confrontation with Kevin. But though she'd known they were both pissed with the man and likely would each have merrily punched his lights out, neither of them had made a move do to so.

Once that pain-in-the-ass had driven off, none of them had spoken of him again. And though they'd both had questions in their eyes, neither Lucas nor Chase had tried to slake their curiosity or pressed for details. Neither of them had done anything to press their advantage or throw their "maleness" in her face. They respected her right to be in charge of her own life.

She really didn't know what to make of them or this relationship they were all having together, except for one thing: she wanted more.

When she was within a few feet of the stream, her lovers stepped out from the shade of the giant maple.

"We've been thinking," Lucas said, and Maddy wondered about the devil in his smile.

"Should I be worried?" she asked.

"Likely," he admitted. He looked at Chase for a moment then turned his attention back to her. The heat in his gaze as his eyes wandered over her immediately lit her fires.

"We both think that one of the 'rules' we should have is in this relationship of ours is balance."

"Balance?"

"Yeah. You know, so that we're all equal here."

Since one of her lines in the metaphorical sand had always been keeping control of her life, and her ranch, she could understand that. If she didn't want anyone tromping all over her individual sphere, she imagined they felt the same. Some women liked to get right in and change the man they had an affair with. She'd never understood that herself. Conversely, her main reason for not wanting a serious relationship was that from what she'd seen most of her life, once you let a man into your bed he thought he had the right to tell you what to do in and out of it. So the idea of balance appealed to her. "That seems more than fair to me," she said.

"Well, good. Because what Chase and I thought is that since you're the boss nine-to-five around here, you ought to give over in the off hours—when it's just the three of us alone together, as lovers."

"Give over?" Hard to string two words together when her body had come awake under such heated stares.

"Well, it's not fair to you, that you should be in charge of everything *all* the time. You need to cut yourself some slack here. No need for you to be in charge of anything when we're alone like this. Is there?"

Maddy had to squeeze her inner muscles to rein in her arousal. Her nipples had begun to tighten, and an achy-empty feeling hummed between her legs, stretching up to the base of her belly.

"No," she agreed, "there's no need for me to be in charge of anything when we're alone like this."

Such an expression of satisfaction filled Lucas' face that she found herself smiling. His next words wiped that smile from her face.

"Then get off that horse, woman, and strip."

Chapter 6

"What did you just say?"

If Lucas didn't know better, he would have been put off by Maddy's tone. But he did know better. He wasn't good at reading most people, but he'd come to know Maddy pretty well over the years.

"You heard me. Get off your horse and strip."

"But the two of you are fully dressed."

That was as close to a pout as he'd ever seen on her face and told him all he needed to know about her mood. She would be more than willing to play along. Lucas gave in to the smile tugging at the corner of his mouth. He made a show of looking down his front, then turning to give Chase the same perusal. "Why, so we are."

Chase stepped forward and grabbed hold of her horse's bridle. Maddy stared at him for another long minute. Then slowly, she swung her right leg over the saddle horn and dismounted.

She used to wear her hair long, and in a braid. But when she'd been eighteen, about a month after he'd hired on, she'd cut her hair short. He'd already had a few fantasies about that glorious blond hair at the time and had been disappointed that she'd shorn it.

I wonder if she'd grow it back, if we asked her to?

"Lose the hat first," he said. He could see she was turned on. Hard to hide those pebbled nipples in that close fitting t-shirt she wore. But he saw hesitation in her eyes, and maybe just a hint of apprehension.

He could attest from very recent experience that a thread of apprehension during foreplay was not a bad thing at all.

Chase had taken Diamond over to where they'd tethered the other horses. But he'd returned, standing right behind Lucas.

"Someday I want her wearing boots and nothing else," Chase murmured loud enough for them all to hear.

"That is an intriguing image," Lucas agreed. "We'll have to add it to that list. But for right now, those boots have to go."

Maddy responded to being spoken about in the third person by raising one eyebrow. But she didn't protest and he judged her willing to see just what he and Chase had in mind. She had a bit of trouble taking off the boots with nothing to balance against, but in short order she stood before them in sock feet.

The heat wave had broken early that morning, leaving the day warm, but not oppressively hot. A light breeze teased the leaves on the trees, and with the rippling of water in the stream formed the only sounds. No bawling cattle, no shouts of men broke the peace of this May afternoon.

They alone occupied this idyll, and Lucas knew their privacy was absolute.

Chase slipped his arms around Lucas from behind, resting his chin on his shoulder. "Can we get rid of the jeans next?" he asked, as he placed a kiss on Lucas's neck.

"Sounds good," Lucas agreed.

If the way Maddy's nipples peaked harder was any indication, she didn't mind the way this scene had begun to play out. He thought her fingers might just be shaking a little as she popped the snap on the denim, pulled the zipper down and peeled the jeans off.

"That really turns me on, t-shirt, undies and socks. Don't know why. Lover, our woman is *hot*."

Lucas could tell it did turn Chase on. The ridge of his erection pressed against Lucas's ass. He felt his own grow in response. Maddy noticed. He saw the flicker in her eyes and could have sworn he could feel the heat of her arousal climbing to match theirs.

"Take your shirt off, Maddy."

"You two are still fully dressed."

Lucas wasn't certain if that was a real protest, or not. Deciding to take things as far to the edge as she would allow, he crossed his arms over his chest. "Do as you're told."

He felt the tension in Chase, and could see it on Maddy. She would have no idea that this would be an important moment. Neither he nor Chase had any desire to dominate this strong, vital woman— well, except in sexy little games, like now. They were, however, determined to play out this scene, and others just like it that they'd discussed.

He waited while she looked at him, then Chase. Finally she crossed her arms in front of herself, grabbing the hem of the shirt in both hands. She had it up and off in a heartbeat.

"Now who would ever expect that under that no-nonsense ranchers' wardrobe, and covering that serious-as-a-heart-attack body there would be come-in-your-pants sexy silk and lace?"

Lucas laughed at Chase's characterizations, delighted that Maddy not only smiled, but looked pleased. "Socks now, woman."

It only took her a moment to slide those off.

"How do you feel right now, Maddy?"

"More than half naked."

When Lucas tilted his head to the side, she got the message that he wanted more than that. "I'm horny. *Very* horny. I want you guys naked so I can look at those gorgeous cocks. Touch them. Taste them."

Oh, she was good. Before Lucas could say anything, Chase thrust his hips against him, his denim-covered rod promising delights, and said, "Now, darlin', we appreciate the dirty talk. But don't you go rushing us, here. We have all afternoon. No need to be in such a hurry."

Maddy's eyes betrayed her laughter. "Can't blame a girl for trying."

"No, indeed," Lucas agreed. "So as a reward for your efforts, you have our permission to take off your bra."

Her gaze met and held his as she reached behind, unhooked the fastener, then dropped the lacy garment to the grass.

"You have pretty breasts," Lucas said, allowing his eyes to roam at will. "Plump, just slightly more than a handful. They taste sweet, too, and when I have your nipple in my mouth, when I feel it swell and harden, I feel ten feet tall. When I suck on your breast, do you feel it pulling at your pussy, does it make you wet?"

"Yes." The single word came out strangled, and Lucas knew he'd aroused her.

"Good job," Chase said. Turning his head he placed another light kiss on Lucas' neck. Then he turned his attention back to Maddy. "Show us."

Uncertainty danced across her face, but only for a moment. She dropped her panties to the ground, then spread her legs slightly.

"Turn around and bend over."

Color washed her face, but she did as he asked.

"You're wet now, woman. Your body is getting ready for us, isn't it? Your hot tunnel is getting ready for us to fuck you, isn't it?" Chase's voice had dropped a notch and Lucas could feel his erection had grown. The tiny spasm that convulsed Maddy's feminine folds said she definitely felt exactly that way.

"*Yes.*"

"Good. Now come here."

* * * *

Maddy didn't know if her legs would continue to hold her. Arousal sang through her body, weakening her knees. Lucas' erection tented the front of his jeans, and oh how she wanted to wrap her hands and lips around it. Both he and Chase looked at her as if she was the most beautiful, most desirable woman in the entire world. She'd never before been so aware of her power as a woman as she was right at that moment. She freely obeyed every command, but she gave up nothing.

When she stopped walking bare inches separated her from her men. Lucas reached out and gently stroked the underside of her left breast. The heat from his touch shot out to every part of her body.

"So soft. So pretty. We have a surprise for you. Do you trust us?"

Trust wasn't a commodity she'd had much use for most of her life. She'd always held people at arm's length. Even her father, whom she'd loved beyond reason had, at times, abused that gift. A woman used to being on her own, she always stood on her own two feet, shouldering every burden and chore alone. In some ways, the concept of trusting someone else ran counter to her instincts.

And yet.

A bond had already formed between the three of them. And of the three of them, these men had extended incredible trust to her already. Here she stood in the great outdoors in the middle of a Sunday afternoon, naked before them like some sort of ceremonial offering. Their eyes promised glorious rewards, and she'd already had a taste of what they could do to her. Did she trust them with her body?

"Yes. Yes, I trust you."

"Good."

Chase stepped back allowing Lucas to take her hand and lead her around to the other side of the large maple.

"What in the world?" Her eyes couldn't at first make sense of the sight.

"It's a hammock."

The hammock had been strung up at about waist height between two branches of one of the sturdy old trees. A white bed sheet covered the netting. As they drew closer, she could see four ropes dangling, two each from either side at the top and bottom of the thing.

Before she could ask what they planned, Chase scooped her up in his arms and laid her on the hammock—cross-ways. The device supported her from the top edge of her ass to her neck.

Lucas immediately appeared at her head. Gasping, she understood the presence of the dangling ropes. In moments her wrists and ankles had been tied to the hammock, and she lay spread-eagle and swinging slightly.

A wave of vulnerability swept her, and the urge to cover herself found her pulling slightly on the ropes.

"We won't hurt you," Lucas promised.

Of course they wouldn't. How could she explain to them that she didn't fear for her safety or well-being, she just felt...exposed? It would sound silly, because they'd both not only seen her naked a few times now, but she doubted there was even one inch of her flesh they hadn't touched.

"This will hold you, baby," Chase added.

And then they began. Gently, Chase ran his hands along the length of her legs, slowly caressing with a touch so light he could have been using a feather. At the same time, Lucas stroked her arms, petting her as she'd seen him pet his gelding. Relaxation settled upon her, everywhere their hands brushed. Her muscles let go, just let go of tension she'd not fully even realized she'd carried. Nature helped, the gentle breeze dancing between her legs, playing across her nipples, so that relaxation began to edge, ever so subtly, into arousal.

The stroke of the breeze against her dewy folds became the brush of fingers. Back and forth, in a rhythm slow and sure, Chase tantalized her woman-flesh and Lucas echoed the touch against her beaded nipples. Both breasts were cupped and squeezed, both nipples captured and pinched at the same time two long, strong fingers entered her.

Maddy closed her eyes and cried out, the spike in arousal so fierce, she lifted her hips into it.

"Now there's an invitation if I ever saw one," Chase whispered, his voice soft, the words puffing warm breath against her intimate flesh. Then he placed his mouth on her.

"Oh, God!" The swirl of tongue and the glide of lips, wet and hot and bold raced her heart and heated her blood.

"Don't come, darlin," Lucas whispered in her ear then tasted her ear with his tongue.

"*Please.*" She didn't care if she begged, the sensation of Chase's mouth on her, of being splayed and played obliterated her thoughts, her will, until she wanted *only* to come.

"Not just yet. Here, darlin'" Lucas turned her head just slightly to the right, and when he fastened his lips on hers, she returned the kiss with everything in her, opening her mouth wide, sucking his tongue, stroking it with hers.

"That's it," he praised, and she opened her eyes to watch him straighten up.

She whimpered and didn't care. As he popped the button and opened the zipper on his pants, she opened her mouth, wanting nothing more than to feel the heat and strength of him between her lips.

"Look how eager you are for my lover's cock. He tastes good, doesn't he, Maddy? So hot and salty and *male*."

Chase had taken his mouth from her but still stroked her drenched pussy with his fingers. His words enflamed her. She *was* eager, not just for Lucas' cock but for his as well.

Lucas approached her head, and Maddy settled her lips on his flesh, sucking strongly until she had him inside her mouth, the flavor of him going straight to her womb. The sound of another zipper drew her gaze to the man now standing between her legs and sliding a condom into place.

Chase stepped forward, and Maddy lifted her hips to his penetration.

They used the motion of the hammock, gently rocking back and forth to aid their loving of her and Maddy thought she would explode with the joy of it, the sheer beauty and the thrill of it. Nothing mattered but this, nothing existed but this.

Who would have thought she'd experience such freedom, essentially having no control? She had given them this, thinking as the ropes tightened around her wrists and ankles that she gave them a gift, but instead she was the beneficiary. The arousal swirled and moved inside her, a beautiful tingly and light feeling that became, in and of itself, the most wondrous pleasure she'd ever experienced. For long moments they communed, she and the arousal that bathed her. And then, just a little, it changed.

Chase's cock stretched her feminine passage, Lucas's cock stretched her mouth. The thrusting heat and brush of hair against her clit matched the salty heat in her mouth and she wanted more, and still more. She wanted her arms free to wrap around one, and her legs free to wrap around the other. She wanted to keep them both inside her and soar.

"Do you want to come, baby?"

She could only groan. No way did she want to let go of Lucas even long enough to answer him.

"I think that's a yes." Chase's voice and Luc's answering chuckle both washed over her.

"Come for us, baby. Come on my cock, while our cocks come inside you." Chase's words commanded her, and her body rushed to obey.

Her climax exploded, the pounding, thrusting, heartbeat of ecstasy, wave after wave of it obliterating everything, every thought, every emotion, until only the hot pulsing, the eruption of salty lust remained. Her throat swallowed, her feminine passage convulsed, as she fed on the rapture of her lovers. The fire of passion consumed her atom by atom, until she had not one ounce of energy, or stress left.

Her body shivered, her lips quivered as the orgasm ebbed, as the aftershocks took over.

"Rest for a while," Lucas whispered as he placed a gentle kiss on her lips. "Just for a while, then Chase and I will trade places. The afternoon is young."

Maddy groaned, and the masculine laughter her lovers offered in response wrapped around her like a blanket as she drifted off to sleep.

Chapter 7

Chase had forgotten how good a wild, hard ride could be.

Ransom, a spirited chestnut gelding, seemed to relish the speed and the freedom, too. Their morning assignment had been to head out to the western-most pasture and check on the number of cattle grazing. A simple assignment, and since they'd secured all the fences, no one expected any of the cows to have escaped. But there could still be predators of the four-legged variety, and Maddy liked each of her three pastures checked on a regular basis.

Chase had traveled far and wide when he'd left here all those years ago. He'd been to a lot of places, done a lot of things, and made a lot of friends. But this place had always shone in his mind as home. He felt so pleased to be here, even if he did occasionally miss a few of his friends.

Thinking of some of those friends now, he pulled his cell phone out of his pocket and dialed all the way to New York.

"Haggerty Investigations."

A grin split his face as the familiar voice echoed in his ear. "Philip, don't tell me you've lost another secretary?"

"Chase! My God, man, where the hell have you been? It's good to hear your voice."

"Yours, too. I've been here and there. But mostly, I decided to come home."

"No shit! You're in Colorado? Good for you. And to answer your first question, no, I have *not* lost another secretary. You'll be pleased to know that I've worked on my one or two very minor personality flaws. Sheila has been with me for nearly two years. She's just gone out for a bit is all."

"Well, good. How's your dad? And Roger?"

Philip Haggerty had filled the role of best friend for a lot of years. His father, Patrick, had more or less adopted Chase when he'd been eighteen. Patrick's confidence and encouragement had resulted in Chase going to college. When he thought back to those days, it still floored him that men like Patrick Haggerty existed in the world. His acceptance of his son's lifestyle remained, in Chase's eyes, truly amazing.

He'd more or less joined the Haggerty clan as Philip's partner then slid to the role of additional son and brother when the romantic relationship between himself and Phil had sputtered to an end.

Philip had met Roger a few months after that, and the two men had been together ever since.

"Dad's great. He's on a cruise right now, touring the Mediterranean. Roger's good too, and I am so glad you called, because we've decided to get married. Roger's family is in Boston, and we're going to have the ceremony there."

"Congratulations!" Chase felt his throat tighten a little. He and Philip held the same cherished dream, though the exact definition for each of them differed slightly. Because of that, while his friend could look forward to formalizing his relationship, Chase knew he would never be able to take that final step. "So when is the wedding?"

"We're waiting until October, because his sister is in England till then and can't shake free. Give me your address there and I'll send you an invitation." There was a pause and Chase caught the slight change in tone. "Do I put the words "and guests" on it?"

"Yeah. We've taken a first step. It just remains to be seen how far we can go. Actually, that's one of the reason's I'm calling, Mister Private Investigator slash lawyer with ties."

"You know I'm here for you. What's up?"

Chase had been having very bad feelings about that visit last week from Kevin Marsh. Something about the guy just rubbed Chase the wrong way. Maddy hadn't spoken of it since, but he wondered if something wasn't going on because she'd seemed a bit off the last day or so.

Everything had been fine Sunday afternoon when they'd all returned, sated and sleepy, from their time by the stream. After dinner, she'd gone into her office, just to check up on e-mail and catch up on ranch business. When she'd come out, she'd been distracted—and, he'd thought at the time, stressed.

Chase didn't know why he believed Marsh lay behind the change in her mood and temperament, but he'd learned to trust his gut instincts. So he gave Philip all the information he had on the man, which admittedly wasn't much.

"I'll get back to you on this. Chase, I'm really glad you called, and I'm very happy you decided to take a chance and go home."

"Thanks. Just wish me luck."

"You know I do."

Chase closed his phone after giving Philip the number at the ranch. Looking around, he took in the majestic beauty of the Rocky Mountains. The air smelled and looked lean and fragrant, in stark contrast to the pollution filled skies of some of the places he'd lived.

He'd taken a degree in accounting and business, but riding the range, working with his hands and his back as well as his brain suited him more. He could be at home on Wall Street, and could mingle with the movers and shakers of the world, but he appreciated the company of a good horse and stalwart pines.

Reining his horse around, he headed back toward home. Lunch time was drawing near, and this afternoon he and Lucas planned to ride into Gunnison for supplies.

Chase grinned again, just thinking about spending some time alone with the man. He'd be asking Lucas to make a stop at the post office. He'd phoned an order in to a specialty shop in New York the week before, and the package should have arrived by now.

* * * *

Just enough trees lined North Main Street in Gunnison to lessen the starkness of the city. Lucas knew this place, of course. Marshville served well for the necessities; especially with its location so close to the ranch. But if you wanted a good meal, or to catch the latest Hollywood flick, then Gunnison would be your destination. It had always been his, he mused as he pulled the ranch truck around the corner so he could enter the parking lot of the ranch supply store. He shot a look over at Chase, who'd been trying to take in everything since they'd arrived in the city.

"Not much compared to some of the places you've lived, I bet," he said as he turned off the engine.

"Size-wise, no. New York is massive. But I don't think I'm cut out for big city living. I hadn't been there more than a few months before I began to itch for wide-open places again."

"Took you long enough to come home." Lucas heard the edge in his voice and wondered why he was trying to pick a fight with the younger man.

"You don't have to be worried that I'll get bored and go away again, Lucas. It's just not going to happen."

Lucas pulled the keys out of the ignition, let his fingers play over them as he inhaled deeply, trying to ease the shaky feeling of relief that had swept over him with Chase's words.

"How do you do that? How do you know so easily what I'm thinking and feeling, when I don't even hardly know myself?" In the short time they'd been lovers, what thrilled Lucas the most—even more than the sex between them and with Maddy—was the way Chase had of *taking care* of him.

"It's a gift."

Lucas laughed, and he heard the edge in the sound. The next moment, Chase's hand touched his. The younger man stroked him then laced fingers with him. Lucas held on and felt solidarity in their connection, an element of warmth and safety Lucas hadn't known he'd hungered for.

"I know because my heart tells me. Yes, I did take a long time to come home. You, Maddy, even the ranch—you were like the shining beacon in my past. The feelings I had for you seemed so huge, but I was afraid that, in my yearning, in my loneliness and my neediness, I'd built them up beyond reality. I feared you couldn't—or wouldn't—let me in."

Lucas felt himself blanch as a terrible possibility crossed his mind. He believed he'd always kept his attraction to men buried. Now he worried if, somehow years ago, he'd said something, done something, he shouldn't have. "You were only a kid. Did I—"

"Of course you didn't. Lucas, you never said or did anything even remotely provocative. You never once betrayed your nature. *That's* why it took so long for me to get up the nerve to come here. What if I'd only imagined what I'd sensed in you? What if I'd only imagined that Maddy might come to care for me, too?"

Lucas met his gaze and held it for a long time. "You're my first," he said slowly. "I didn't want to admit even to myself that I felt attraction to *both* men and women. But there've been a couple of times in the past when I've met men I sensed might be interested in me. I could have become involved with them. I know it now, and I think I knew it then. I tuned them out. But with you, that option never even occurred to me."

"So maybe we've both found our place," Chase said quietly.

"God, I hope so." Lucas closed his eyes for one moment. More than anything, he wanted to hang on to this feeling of belonging that had begun to fill him since the afternoon Chase had knocked on his screen door.

When he opened his eyes again, he offered Chase a smile. "The sooner we can get things done, the sooner we can get home. Maybe we can talk Maddy into playing. Or maybe we can steal a little time to ourselves."

"My thoughts, exactly. But we have to swing by the post office. There should be a package there for me."

"Oh yeah?" Lucas got out of the truck and looked over at Chase, whose Cheshire-cat grin made him smile in turn.

"Yeah. I ordered a few toys—items designed to liven things up in the bedroom for us all."

"Things get much livelier in the bedroom and I may die of a heart attack."

It pleased Lucas enormously that he could make Chase laugh.

* * * *

Arabella, a two year old chestnut filly, could be a handful. Maddy had bought her dam Annabel at auction, one of only four horses she'd purchased in the first year she branched out into the horse business.

Maddy's father had been a cattleman through and through, and proud of it. But Maddy didn't judge the future of beef to be all that sound. One of the problems was BSE—otherwise known as mad cow disease—popping up with enough regularity that anyone whose entire livelihood came from beef cattle took one hell of a chance. Not so likely, really, that any of *her* cattle would be struck with that disease; but any outbreak in the United States, even if only one or two cows and hundreds of miles away, could tighten the market right up for everyone. So three years ago Maddy had decided to diversify and implement a horse breeding program as a way of supplementing the cattle income for the ranch.

Arabella balked at the paces Maddy tried to teach her. She'd much rather just run wild than learn how to take direction. Maddy couldn't really blame her, but she held firm to the reins, and waited the fractious mare out. Her horse breeding program had begun to do well. She had three mares and one gelding ready to show some prospective buyers next week, and another potential customer had shown interest in Arabella. Snagging that business would be a real coup for her.

The Lassiters from over near Barstow wanted to add to their cutting stock. They'd already begun making a name for themselves at the futurities. A few good customers like them would go a long way toward giving Maddy the credentials she needed to become a known name in breeding circles. Arabella had excellent blood lines. Her dam and sire had both been champions. Maddy again waited for the filly to obey commands. The Lassiters—if they bought Arabella—would want to saddle train her themselves, and then train her for cutting. But the horse still had to be amenable to being led.

There existed a good market for cutters and saddle horses. Her father had never fully approved, but she loved working with the horses. Why shouldn't she earn her living by doing what she loved rather than by what had always been traditional?

Traditional. *There's an interesting word.* At the moment, her personal life could be called anything but traditional. She was having a flaming hot affair with two men at the same time. Two men who were also having a flaming hot affair with each other.

Some moments Maddy had trouble getting her head around the entire situation. And then there came the other moments—not just times when they lay sprawled naked together, sated and teetering on the edge of sleep—but times when the three of them just shared the evening paper on the front porch, or had their morning coffee together, that she thought she might be the luckiest woman in the world.

She'd sent her men off to Gunnison. It was difficult for them to find time to be alone together. She very much wanted to afford them the opportunity to do just that. Both Lucas and Chase wanted to be discreet. Maddy sensed that Chase would be perfectly comfortable if his relationship with Lucas became known, but she suspected Lucas wasn't quite there yet. She knew Chase was his first male lover.

She hadn't told either of her men, but she'd already resolved if anyone on her ranch gave them grief, that sorry s.o.b. would be sent packing. She had no tolerance for hate or discrimination of any kind.

The sound of tires on dirt caught her attention, and she looked over her shoulder. *Damn it.* She would have thought after the blistering response she'd given his e-mail request to meet last Sunday that Kevin Marsh would have gotten the message that she had no interest in having any contact with him at all.

If he thinks I'm going to drop everything for him, he has another think coming. She continued to work with the mare, though both she and the horse knew it wasn't as serious a session as it had been only a few moments before.

"That horse would obey you better if you took a crop to it."

If he'd been looking for words that would piss her off, he couldn't have chosen better. "Now that is exactly the kind of thing I would expect you to say, Marsh. Why don't you just go to hell? And get off my land, while you're at it."

"You want to be careful how you respond to me, Maddy. Our life together will run much more smoothly once you learn your place. That's something I think I'm going to enjoy teaching you. And I won't hesitate to use a crop in the teaching. Or my belt. Matter of fact, I think I'm looking forward to that part."

Maddy felt a shiver along her skin. Despite the fact that she had absolute faith in her ability to take care of herself, she wished for one moment that her two men had returned from the city. Hell, she wished the rest of her crew were within ear-shot. *Not the time to give in to skittishness.* The first lesson she'd ever learned in dealing with untrained animals she applied now. Never show your fear.

She turned around, keeping her hold on the horse. "Damn, Kevin. You've gone right loco if you think for one moment that you and I are going to have any kind of *life* together."

"I think you're going to change your mind. I truly do. Because if you don't, why, your life is going to become a real living hell for you. With my help of course."

She hadn't seen the large manila envelope in his hands. Now he raised it and pulled out the contents. She could tell just by the look of what he held he had a photograph of some sort. *Oh God.* Her heart thudded in her chest as she wondered if this slime-bucket had somehow snuck onto her land last Sunday...she swallowed hard, determined to appear unmoved.

"Met a man last Saturday night all the way over in Colorado Springs," he began slowly.

Maddy frowned. Colorado Springs?

"Man by the name of Neil Crawford," Marsh continued. "Doesn't ring any bells, does it? That's because you never met him. You are, however, acquainted with an employee of one of his business competitors. And as luck would have it—my good luck, and your bad luck, in my opinion—Mr. Crawford had engaged in video surveillance of his competition. He set his rival up for a police sting. Turned out pretty good for him, by the way. State cops moved in, cleared out the other guy's organization."

Maddy had begun to relax when she realized that Marsh *hadn't* stooped to the lowest form of voyeurism. But as he'd continued to speak, her heart began hammering in her chest again in slow, painful beats.

"The State's Attorney General gave a news conference, actually, about the successful sting operation the state police conducted. He's quite proud of getting hundreds of thousands of dollars in illegal substances off the streets. And he's vowed—and it's very handy that this just happens to be an election year—to make sure the 'mop up operation' is thorough and complete. I find him to be a self-righteous son-of-a-bitch, personally. But that won't prevent me from sending this photograph to him, and the local news outlets, with all the pertinent data, such as your name and address. Only one thing will prevent me from doing that, and it's all up to you."

Marsh extended the photo he held, and with a sense of sinking dread, Maddy reached out to take it. She didn't want to look, but knew she had to.

The lighting was very good, considering the picture had been taken late at night. The scene depicted a street corner in Colorado Springs, just an ordinary street corner on the edge of a less than fashionable neighborhood. The picture had captured a man and a woman, so obviously doing business. The man held out a bag filled with white pills. The woman offered a stack of cash in exchange.

Five hundred dollars, Maddy thought now. Five hundred dollars once a month for nearly a year.

Because of the angle taken by the photographer, both faces—the male seller and the female buyer—were not only visible, but recognizable.

Maddy gazed at her own image, stark and damning, and wondered what in the hell she was going to do now.

Chapter 8

He'd very nearly said the words.

Chase went through the motions of cleaning the tack, his mind not on his work, but the day's trip to town.

Sitting alone with Lucas in the parking lot of that supply store, Chase had very nearly laid himself bare, emotionally. He'd only ever said those words once before in his entire life, and he'd never once heard them back. Maybe to other men, the words 'I love you' didn't matter that much. Maybe other men could say them, and it didn't matter if they meant them or not.

But they mattered to Chase. Saying the words had opened him, and when they'd been thrown back in his face, the wound had cut deep and taken a very long time to heal.

His mother certainly thrived on hearing those words, at least from the men she'd brought to her bed. Now, as an adult who hungered for those very words himself, he didn't know if he could blame her for that. There lived a need inside the human heart, a need so great that sometimes it eclipsed all other needs: the need to be loved. But to Chase that need meant more than being loved; it meant being accepted for who and what he was, and *belonging*. It meant the sure and certain knowledge that no matter what, you would never be alone again. And it was the glorious freedom to love, to declare that love, to *give*. Chase thought that it just might be more important for the heart to be able to give love, than to receive it.

Chase couldn't blame his mother for wanting to have all that. He wanted it himself. But wanting and needing so desperately left him nervous of taking a chance, being the first one to say those words now. Just in case he didn't hear them back.

Chase knew he was in love with Lucas, and he felt pretty sure he was in love with Maddy, too. But he wouldn't say the words to them. At least, not for a while. Besides, this relationship of theirs had just begun. They hadn't yet found their place in it, discovered their boundaries and were still discovering each other. Lots of time for declarations to be made.

"So what happened in town today? Lucas meet a hot babe or something?"

Charlie stood at the door to the tack room, his clothes drenched with sweat and caked with dust. He'd heard the man come into the barn a few moments before, but hadn't expected conversation.

"What makes you ask that?" Chase kept a smile on his face, even though the question had unnerved him. He'd met all types in his life, and he'd recognized Charlie straight off. The kind of man that men like Chase tended to avoid, he was the type that could be generally mouthy and brave only after downing a couple of six packs and surrounded by a dozen of their close friends. Men like Charlie had given him more grief in the past than he cared to think about.

"Man's walking around with a smile on his face like he's anticipating some prime pussy real soon."

"Is that right? I can't say I noticed—either the smile, or whether or not he met someone."

"Or maybe you're just jealous."

"Jealous?" Chase felt a definite chill race up his spine in response to the jeering tone. Maybe Charlie was just teasing, and maybe his words signaled a more onerous attitude.

"Hot babe goes for the old fart instead of the young stud. Sure as hell would piss me off, I don't mind telling you. Crap, Luc hasn't gotten laid in so long, he likely can't even get it up anymore."

Chase felt his temper soar fast and hot. *Careful.* He had to choose his words carefully. Not for himself—he didn't mind taking on a walking bullshit artist like Charlie—but he had to be careful not to do or say anything that would make Lucas uncomfortable.

"I'd appreciate it if you'd not speak unkindly of Lucas."

"Yeah, old Bill said you grew up on this place. So you'd probably know if Luc ever banged Maddy. I like to think he did. Talk in town is that she's a dyke. Now that would be a waste. She sure has a fine set of knockers on her. Wouldn't mind giving that filly a hot ride myself."

Chase set down the bridle he'd been cleaning and turned around slowly. *I always thought the expression 'seeing red' was only a cliché. Who knew?* "What is it with you? What's this fascination with other people's sex lives?"

Charlie must have caught a glimpse of Chase's temper because his demeanor immediately changed.

"Don't mean nothing by it, Chase. Just guy talk, that's all. You work with people, and you wonder, you know?"

"Well, do yourself a favor. Don't share any more of that kind of guy talk where I can hear it. Because I have way too much respect for both Luc and Maddy to give you a pass on it a second time."

Chase had to wait long minutes after Charlie slunk off before he dared head over to the bunk house for dinner. If nothing else, that pleasant exchange told him one thing for certain.

In New York, or any other large city he'd been in, there would be no problem living openly with his lovers. But rural Colorado was more than hundreds of miles away from New York; it was a world away. And any hope he had of being open in his relationships here had just been shot all to hell. He didn't mind if people gossiped about him. But he wouldn't expose the ones he loved to that kind of derision in their own hometown.

* * * *

"I'm going to take a shower."

Maddy tossed down the paper, got to her feet, and nearly stomped into the house. Lucas looked over at Chase. "She's in a mood."

"Yeah, that was a 'fuck off and leave me alone kind of exit'." Chase set his portion of the paper down on the chair Maddy had just vacated.

"I'm no good with this relationship stuff. I figure there are times when a person needs to be alone, take some time to themselves, and it's okay if they're pissed off. Is this one of those times?" he asked.

Chase reached over and ran a hand down Lucas' arm. He'd always maintained that he'd never been one for displays of affection. None of the women he'd ever dated had looked closely enough to see that, in fact, he was. The small touches that Chase lavished on him made him feel cherished, an amazing feeling.

"I don't think so. She's been in a mood since dinner. Distracted. Edgy. Do you have any idea why?" Chase asked.

"Bill mentioned he saw Marsh's car driving off this afternoon. That could be it."

"Marsh again."

"Yeah. Something about that guy rubs me wrong, but that's nothing compared to the way Maddy seems to react to him." Lucas felt restless. Getting to his feet, he paced over to the railing.

The sun hung low on the horizon, the day nearly done. He could see the very edge of the paddock, the near pasture, and the tall mountains beyond. He loved this area, couldn't imagine himself living anywhere else.

"We're going to have to get her to talk about it," Chase said from close behind him.

"She can be as stubborn as two mules when she has a mind to."

"Yeah, I think I figured that one out already."

Lucas felt the heat of Chase's body, and when the younger man stepped close, Lucas gave in to temptation and leaned against him just slightly. He was rewarded with a gentle caress against his back that evolved into a small hug.

"I have faith in our ability to worm the truth out of her when she's good and wrecked from our very thorough attention. Speaking of which," Chase stepped back after giving Lucas one more caress. "Why don't you go in and help Maddy with her shower? I'm going to go and grab that parcel I left in your kitchen."

Chase hadn't elaborated on what was in that box he'd picked up at the post office that afternoon. The box itself held no clues, wrapped only in unmarked brown paper. But just recalling what Chase had said earlier—the contents would liven things up in the bedroom—got his juices flowing. Coupled with the image of Maddy, wet and naked in the shower, Lucas felt his cock hardening.

"Yeah, why don't I?" He took a moment to watch one lover walk away before heading inside the house to his other one.

* * * *

He stepped back into the shadows of the barn. He'd been frozen in place as the tableau had unfolded before him. Even now, a thread of disbelief wove its way through his thoughts—his mind trying to say that what his eyes had just seen was not real.

In the next instant, the rising tide of anger belayed that. His eyes hadn't deceived him, but obviously *they* had.

There was a word for their kind, a word he could still hear his daddy spit, a word that made his flesh crawl.

Faggots.

Two faggots lived right here, on the Circle D. His belly burned with instant hatred. They lived on *his* ranch, tainting everything they touched. One of them slept in the bunkhouse, where he slept. Mother of God, what if Chase came on to him in the night?

Hidden in the shadows, he stood and watched as Chase walked, free as you please, into Lucas' house. He flicked his eyes to the front porch of the homestead, but Lucas was no longer in sight. He must have gone inside the house.

He kept his eyes on the man as Chase walked out of Lucas' place, back towards Maddy's. He felt his anger rise as the bastard opened the door and went straight on in without so much as a knock on the door or a by-your-leave.

He waited, waited, but no one came back out. Darkness descended and he shook himself, wondering how long he'd just stood there watching. He turned, walked slowly toward the bunkhouse. He wouldn't tell the others what he'd just seen. Hell, just thinking of those two gay boys together made him want to puke.

Puking wasn't the answer, though. Something had to be done. He didn't know what, but he'd think on it.

Someone had to teach those faggots a lesson.

* * * *

Maddy braced herself against the tiles, her arms outstretched, head bowed, and let the hot water beat down on the back of her neck. Stress sat in a heavy knot at the top of her spine, grinding away at her muscles and her spirit.

From the moment Kevin Marsh had dropped his ultimatum that afternoon, the tension had been building.

"I'm going to be generous, Maddy. You've got till Sunday. That's four days. You come to me and agree to get married, and sign the ranch over to me, and this picture goes away. You don't, and I'm dropping the biggest dime of all time. Expect you won't like the inside of a jail cell much."

No way in hell she wanted to marry that bastard. But if he made good on his threat—and she had to believe he would—she'd end up losing not only her freedom, but the ranch, and likely the respect of everyone she knew.

Maddy didn't know what to do.

Her mind was so busy she didn't hear a sound until the shower curtain moved. Two strong hands slid around her body, cupping her breasts, squeezing gently.

Lucas. Amazing how she could tell them apart, just by their touch.

"Thought I'd wash your back for you."

"That's not my back. And I'm not in the mood tonight, Lucas."

"Why, you're right, it's not your back. My mistake. Oh, well, just give me a minute and I bet you'll be in the mood quick enough."

He kept his left hand on her breast. His right slicked around to her side, then slithered down, over her hip, before moving around to her ass and then dipping between her legs. Two fingers slid inside her while his thumb tickled her clit. She gave up the idea of not being in the mood.

"Ah…that's not my back either." She could barely get the words out, so high had her arousal spiked. Still braced by her hands against the shower wall, she pumped her hips in concert with his thrusts, his long, strong fingers going deep, but not nearly deep enough.

Lucas' laughter, soft and smooth, stroked her fires.

"Like that, do you? Let's see what else I can do to get you in the mood."

His hand left her for just a moment, returning with the bar of soap. The addition turned his touch silky, so that everywhere he rubbed came alive with need. Using his thumb, he traced a line along the crack of her ass, pushing lightly against her anus and Maddy damn near shot from the shower. The explosion of sensation startled her.

"What did you just do?" She couldn't stop herself from rubbing against his hand, seeking more.

"Mmm," his response sounded less than enlightening.

He did it again, pressing a little harder against her anus, stretching two long fingers to brush against her clit at the same time and Maddy came, the orgasm so sharp and fierce she cried out. If not for Lucas's arm around her, his hand on her breast, she might have collapsed into a puddle on the floor. On and on the snap and sizzle abraded her nerves and tingled her toes. He kept the stimulation up until she shivered. Then he gathered her close, and used the shower wand to rinse her.

"*Oh, God.*" She felt weak as a kitten and could barely straighten up.

The shower curtain opened completely. Chase stood, naked, with a towel ready. "That sounded like a good one."

"Yeah, one of us had a good one."

"Don't worry, lover, you'll get yours, too. Let me have her."

"Right here, you know," Maddy muttered, annoyed that they would talk about her as if she wasn't.

"Glad to hear it, because we have plans for you."

He wrapped the towel around her and lifted her out of Lucas' arms. She did think it unfair that she had no strength left in her legs to hold herself up. Her head rested for a moment on Chase's shoulder, and he hugged her in turn.

Chase made quick work of drying her, and then dropping the towel, turned her around to face the long vanity.

"Lean against the counter, sweetheart."

"Why?"

He didn't answer her, just laid a hand on her ass and began to massage her. "Spread your legs a little more, and bend over a bit."

His touch between her legs gentle, his fingers probed. She didn't think her sensitive flesh could take more, but she felt the wetness of her rekindled appetite.

"Open that for me, will you, Lucas?"

She heard the sound of a jar being opened. Before she could blink, Chase's hand left her. When it returned, she felt the glide of something slick and chilled against her ass. He stroked over her tiny rosebud, making her pussy clench in desire.

Then slowly he inserted a finger into her.

"One day, soon, you're going to have both our cocks inside you, baby. You'll ride us both and pleasure us all. It's going to hurt a little. Less, if we prepare you properly."

No one had ever done this to her, inserted anything into her ass. As Chase moved his finger in and out, she whimpered, the hunger for more surging as she thrust back, trying to increase the sensations.

"Put some on the pink one. Good."

"Pink one?" Pink one what? Bent over, she couldn't see much of what was going on around her.

"Our lover bought some toys," Lucas said. She could tell he'd moved beside them, but couldn't see what he did.

"Toys?" She knew they existed, of course. The last time she'd ordered a dildo from an online sex shop, she'd perused the other items the company sold. Some had intrigued her, and some had scared the freaking hell out of her.

"Butt plugs. Two pink—for you, and two blue—for Lucas. I'm guess I'm just a traditional kind of guy."

"Two?"

"Two different sizes. You'll wear the small one, first. Help stretch you just a little."

He worked his finger in and out of her, the sensation more than pleasant. Lucas stepped beside her, and she felt his hand on her bottom, sliding down then stroking her slit, finding her clit and rubbing.

"*Please.*" She felt at the mercy of these two men but curiously free. She'd already come once, but her body needed more. The urgency built in her at lightning speed. She tried to work her hips faster, but was held still by masculine hands, her intimate passages prodded by masculine fingers, and could only take what she was being given.

Sounds communicated motion, but made little sense. The jar lid twisted back on. A foil packet torn open.

"I'll put that on for you."

"No, love. Keep your hand on her. Keep it there until I tell you to move it. I want you to feel me fucking her."

Bossy. Before she could draw another breath, she felt something hot and hard and sheathed slide into her pussy. *Chase.* It wasn't only the touch of her men's hands she'd learned. He moved in and out of her with a smooth rhythm that fed her fires. Lucas's fingers splayed across her clit, rubbing gently.

"Mmm. Petting both of you at once. I like that. I like it a lot."

"So do I. I love feeling you stroke my cock as I move in and out of her. When she starts to come, insert that butt plug in one slow, smooth move."

Right here. She wanted to say the words but her breathing hitched as every part of her body began to liquefy. She bent forward more, felt her lips widen to accept whatever was offered, as her heart raced and her blood pounded, as her body was plundered by Chase's energetic cock.

He hit her cervix and she cried out, the slight pain somehow heightening every sensation, until she could only reach for more.

"You're both hot, and getting hotter. I can feel it on my hand, Hot and hard and juicy."

She caught the marvel in Lucas' voice, his groan of desire. He stood close enough, right beside her. Nearly frantic, needing to give as well as take, she turned her head, stuck out her tongue, and teased his cock.

He pushed his hips forward and her lips captured him, her mouth greedy for his taste.

"Mm, yes. *Yes.* Suck me, sweetheart."

Thought ended. Only sensation existed, only arousal, and a driving, burning need for completion. When the first tendrils of her climax sparked to life, Maddy moaned, and sucked on Lucas' cock even more enthusiastically as she tilted her hips just that little bit more.

The starburst of orgasm ignited over her, and as she gave herself to it, Lucas moved his other hand and a soft-hard knob pressed against her anus. Slow, steady, the plug opened her rosebud and began to slide inside her.

The sensation of the double penetration pushed her off the cliff, the pulsing within both sets of lips signaling both men were right there with her. Together they came with a fiery passion she hoped would never end.

Chapter 9

It was a strange sensation, standing quietly while two strangers examined her child, preparing to pass judgment on her.

A lump formed in Maddy's throat. She'd sold a few horses so far, but none of them had been as special to her as Arabella. *Suck it up. This is what the horse breeding business is all about.* Plus, these were the Lassiters. This family had already made a name for itself as trainers and breeders of champion cutting horses. Claiming them as clients would be huge.

Maddy had been under the impression that the championship trainers were a husband and wife team. Husband *had* come along, and stood next to her as the team—his wife and his brother—examined the mare.

"She's a Morgan," Rafe Lassiter said, his manner relaxed as he leaned against the paddock railing next to her.

Maddy turned her attention to him and responded to his easy smile. "She is, and it comes down from both sides. Her dam is Annabel, bred out of the Chamberlain Bay Ranch of Texas. She traces her Morgan blood lines back to Woodbury, one of the original Justin Morgan sons. Her sire is Desperate Wager, owned by the Kinsmores."

"Outside of Boulder," Rafe said, returning his focus on his wife.

"Yes. Her dam has the stronger Morgan links. Her sire is more Quarter Horse, and with a trace of Arabian thrown in for good measure."

Arabella chose that moment to nod her head and put her face into Mrs. Lassiter's hands. Maddy felt that lump burning and swallowed it back. It looked like her little girl had already taken to the woman.

"Your wife has a way with horses. She's already got a reputation as a champion trainer. Is she a whisperer?"

"Not by training, just by nature. Hard to believe my Becca sat her first horse only three years ago."

Three years? "I'm speechless."

Rafe's grin flashed. "Most people are. Travis and I were more or less born to the saddle. Becca was born *for* it."

The two Lassiters in the paddock examining Arabella stood back, speaking quietly.

The woman—Becca—turned away and approached.

"She's a beauty."

"She is." Maddy felt what she imagined to be maternal pride swelling inside her. This *was* the reason she'd gone into the horse business. She looked at Arabella and knew this horse had been destined to make her mark. She imagined that in the hands of a proven trainer like Rebecca Lassiter, Arabella would become the champion she deserved to be. Time, now, to help make that happen.

"She's got tremendous spirit in her; I can tell you right now she'd much rather run than work."

Rebecca Lassiter laughed. "Well, so would I, come to that."

Her brother-in-law joined them. Travis Lassiter seemed the quiet sort. The Lassiter men had obviously been blessed with superior genes. If Maddy wasn't already involved she'd consider flirting with him.

"She's only had minimal training?" he asked.

"I've introduced her to halter and lead, but not saddle."

"She's beautiful. Her dam is Annabel? I nearly bought that horse three years ago. I had just begun to put together our training program, then."

"Horse people. Small world." Maddy smiled. She found herself liking all three Lassiters.

"It is indeed," Travis agreed. "So much so that I have to ask, is that Knight Shadow you have over in the other paddock?"

"You have a good eye, Mr. Lassiter. He's standing stud for three of my ladies."

"We'd be interested in the results of that. You have good stock, Ms. Dalton, and from what I've seen a good hand for breeding. We've got our own program, but we're interested in keeping variety in the blood lines."

That was high praise coming from someone as well established as Travis Lassiter. They knew the price she wanted for Arabella, had known it before taking the trouble to come and look at the horse. Now, though it did tug at her heart, Maddy closed the deal.

"Would you care for some coffee?" They'd have to go up to the house anyway and do the paper work.

"I'd love some," Rebecca said, pre-empting the men.

Maddy could see Travis had more interest in his surroundings and her breeding program than in a cup of coffee. She looked over toward the foaling barn. Chase had come out of it and would be on his way to saddling up and joining Charlie and Pat in the middle pasture. She raised her hand to get his attention.

His ready smile got her insides fluttering. He joined them, nodding and shaking hands as she introduced him to her guests.

"Do you have time to show Travis around? He and his sister-in-law just bought Arabella for their cutting business. He noticed Shadow visiting us and is interested in our program."

"Be glad to, Maddy."

"Appreciate the kindness, Ms. Dalton."

"Maddy, please. Come on up to the house when you're done. I had our cook throw together some snacks, and the coffee is fresh."

* * * *

Chase didn't say anything for a long moment, instead waiting for Maddy and the others to get out of earshot. He'd recognized the man as he'd approached, of course. Not knowing the entire context of his presence, he'd kept the recognition off his face. He tried to think of a good first line, but Travis beat him to the punch.

"I just finished agreeing with Maddy that it was a small world, and damned if that isn't an understatement. Are you on assignment here?"

Chase smiled. "No. I was about to ask you the same thing until Maddy explained. This is home for me. I only worked for the government for a couple of years. While it seemed an interesting career move at the time, I discovered it wasn't the career for me. I never connected you to the Lassiters Maddy mentioned. Are you still on the job?"

"Resigned when my dad died so I could come home and help my brothers run the ranch. Missed the open range. Then I got elected sheriff in Barstow a couple years ago."

"Once a lawman, always a lawman—and this way, you get to have both worlds."

"More or less. Does your woman know you did some undercover work for Uncle Sam?"

It didn't surprise Chase that Travis had picked up on the vibes between him and Maddy. Travis Lassiter was one of the sharpest men he'd ever met. So sharp, that Travis gave him a look that said he knew where Chase was coming from completely. That kind of awareness on the part of others had never been a threat to Chase. "Haven't mentioned it yet. I may end up having to, though, as I asked a friend who also happens to be a former colleague for a favor."

"Oh yeah? Trouble?"

"You want that tour? I can fill you in as we walk."

"Sure, might as well."

Chase gave Travis many of the same details he'd shared with Philip, because in his opinion you could never have too much potential back-up. He and Lucas had both asked Maddy last night what was bothering her. She'd waved off their concerns, denying anything was amiss. They both knew something had to be because she never once mentioned Marsh's visit yesterday afternoon.

He understood her need to be in control of her life, even appreciated to some extent that the need had driven her to be so circumspect. From what Lucas had told him, she'd had to carry too heavy a load all by herself for far too long. There'd been times in the past when she'd depended on her father to do certain things only to have him let her down. Or worse, the man had on occasion created new problems that had nearly had disastrous consequences. In short, in his later years her father had been a huge burden on her ability to cope with the day-to-day running of the ranch. She'd learned that things got done quicker and better if she just did them herself.

Maddy needed to learn that she could lean on Chase and Luc a little. She needed to understand they would never let her down. That would take time. But he didn't think it wise to let her get away with lying to them.

"You've met the man. How did you read him?" Lassiter asked, speaking of Marsh.

"Pure bully. He wants something, that's a given. I'm hoping there's something somewhere we can use as leverage to get him to back off and leave her alone."

"Well, if he's a bully he likely has a string of victims behind him."

"Yeah, that's what I'm thinking."

Chase introduced Travis to the three mares that comprised the latest phase of Maddy's breeding program. Francesca was already likely pregnant and the other two mares had been scheduled to be serviced in the next few days. Both Moon Dancer and Selestial had strong bloodlines that showed in their straight clean legs, and beautiful confirmation. Moon Dancer was a glistening chestnut, Selestial a dazzling black.

"Her dad made his name as a cattleman, but Maddy's heart is with her horses. We're still maintaining a cattle operation, but she believes diversification is the key to survival."

"Well, she's got you in her corner. What did they call you on Wall Street? Mr. Magic? I do know you're a genius at financial structure and planning, which is what made you so valuable for that undercover Op with Treasury."

Chase shook his head. If he didn't know better, he'd say Travis Lassiter was flirting with him. But he *did* know better because Travis was as straight as they came, so he just laughed. "Maddy knows I have an MBA and that I worked in New York, but that's the extent of it."

"Well, my lips are sealed. Reckon we'd best head up to the house. If you like, I can put out my own feelers with regard to Kevin Marsh. See what I come up with."

"Appreciate that. He might just be a persistent little prick who needs nothing more than to be put in his place. But something about him raised my hackles."

"Never discount instincts," Lassiter advised as they headed toward the ranch house.

"Words to live by," Chase agreed.

* * * *

Something was bothering her men. That thought penetrated Maddy's consciousness as she watched Chase and Lucas play at eating their dinner.

She'd been so flushed with her success that afternoon—the money she'd gotten for Arabella had been a hefty amount—that she'd actually cooked dinner in her kitchen for the three of them.

It wasn't something she'd likely do too often. Especially with Chase around because he was a much better cook than she. But Maddy had wanted a small celebration with the two people who meant the most to her. So she'd told Bill she needed to have a meeting with Luc and Chase and to not bother holding dinner for them. He'd grumbled, of course, but then he always did. There'd been times in the last few months especially when she had needed to sit with her foreman and discuss ranch business. Because they were short handed, dinner had proven the best time of day to do that.

Maddy looked up from her food, her eyes moving from Luc to Chase. Something was definitely off with them. She didn't think they'd had a fight, or anything like that. They didn't seem to have any problem *between* them.

Considering all she had on her mind at the moment—parting with a horse she'd raised since birth and Kevin Marsh's ugly ultimatum never from her thoughts—she thought it a testament to her feelings for the both of them that she noticed their moods.

Her first and only instinct was to do whatever she could to fix whatever troubled them.

Was that love?

The few men she'd dated in the past had left her thoughts the moment they left her sight. She had her life, her responsibilities and her work, and anything else had always been secondary. She controlled her own life, and really had never given a good deep damn for anyone or anything else.

Until now.

Now she thought of these two men often—Lucas with his quiet, strong manner and Chase with his sometimes brash boldness. They represented a contrast in personalities, no doubt about it. And each of them fed a need in her. Each of them, in his way, completed her.

Chase made her laugh, dared the hidden child in her to play, to reach and touch and feel. Lucas comforted and nurtured that part of her that felt battered by life and the world in general. In them, with them, she felt connected and included in a way she never had with anyone before.

Oh God, she *was* in love with them both!

"You want to tell us what's been up your ass for the last couple of days?"

That question from Chase startled her, made her blink. His voice held an edge that spoke of having reached a limit of some sort. "Excuse me?"

"You heard the question. We're not hearing the answer." Lucas sounded equally miffed. Maddy felt totally confused.

"Me? I was just wondering what was bothering the two of you!"

"What's bothering us is what's bothering you. Chase said it. You've been upset since we came back from Gunnison the other day. Care to tell us why?"

Maddy felt her heart thud in her chest. She thought she'd been better at hiding her emotions than that. The hair on the back of her neck began to bristle. She wasn't used to having anyone question her in the way these two seemed determined to. She might love them but that didn't give them the right to ride roughshod over her. She was entitled to some privacy, wasn't she?

Still, the feelings she had for them did temper her response. "It's nothing, really," she lied. "Marsh paid me another visit, and I let it get to me. He's just one of those people—he can push my buttons and get under my skin faster than anyone I've ever met. I guess I've just got to develop a thicker skin."

"I see."

And in those two words Lucas conveyed a wealth of disappointment that made Maddy's chest hurt. He leveled a look at her and she wanted to crawl under the table. He looked away from her and said, only, "Chase?"

The younger man pushed back from the table and left the kitchen. She didn't even have time to wonder where he went when he returned, a brown envelop in his hands.

Everything inside Maddy froze with fear and shame. Recognizing the envelop Kevin had given her she slowly got to her feet. "You had no right to invade my privacy!"

Chase simply raised one eyebrow. "This afternoon, you asked me to put the file on Arabella in your office while you showed the

Lassiters out. When the drawer to the filing cabinet closed, this fell off the top, and the photograph slid out. I fully intended to simply slide it back inside. Until I caught a glimpse of it. I know a surveillance photograph when I see one. And I know a drug deal in progress when I see one. And, being the clever person that I am I put two and two together and figured out that Marsh gave you this the other day. You want to tell us what the hell is going on here?"

Maddy didn't think she imagined the derisive tone in Chase's voice. She looked from him to Lucas, and felt her belly clutch. In the face of their disapproval, everything inside her froze. It looked and felt as if they were standing in judgment of her.

"You think I deal drugs?" The outrage exploded from her, drowning out the pain of their expressions, chasing every other emotion away.

"Do we look stupid? We *know* you don't deal drugs. What we're waiting to hear is what this is all about."

Lucas didn't even look at the photo, which meant Chase must have told him about it. They'd been discussing her personal business behind her back, and they had no right to do that.

"It's none of your business." The words came easily, the attitude a comfortable friend. She was in a mess and had no idea what the hell to do about it, but she didn't expect—couldn't expect—anyone to get her out of it but herself. And she sure as hell didn't want anyone telling her what to do as if she was some sort of brainless twit who couldn't even manage her own life. She sure as hell didn't want these men throwing their testosterone-laden weight around as if her having taken them to her bed gave them the right to run her life.

"The hell it isn't our business!" Lucas got to his feet and she didn't think she'd ever seen him so angry. "*You* are our business, lady, everything about you is our business. Don't you know that by now?"

"Just because we have sex doesn't give you the right to run my life!"

"Is that all we are to you, Maddy, really? A couple of cocks that you can use when the urge strikes, and nothing more? People you can fuck when you're horny but be kept in their place otherwise?"

Outrage wasn't only hers, she could see that now. The look of it on Chase as he stood yelling at her cut right through her, to her very heart. *Knee-jerk.* She let her temper and her ego get in the way of her brain. Chase's words shamed her.

"No! I've *never* thought that. You don't understand! This doesn't have anything to do with you—with us. This is *personal.* This is something I have to handle alone."

"You're the one who doesn't understand, Maddy. You don't understand anything at all. But you know where you can find us when you figure it out. Come on, Chase. We're out of here."

Maddy's jaw dropped, the vehemence in Lucas' voice so uncharacteristic she still wasn't certain she'd heard him correctly. If appearances counted for anything, Chase looked just as shocked by Luc's boldness. He looked for one moment as if he might say something more. Instead he nodded, tossed the photograph and envelope onto the table, and followed the older man out.

The kitchen door slammed behind them. The sudden silence after the roar of raised voices felt barren. The quiet wrapped around Maddy but brought no real comfort. She lowered herself to her chair and reached for the discarded photograph.

Not until the image in front of her blurred did she realize she was crying.

Chapter 10

"I'd like to toss her over my knee and spank the living daylights out of her. How can she be so thick headed? *It has nothing to do with us*! How can she say that? What the hell is the *matter* with that woman?" Lucas paced the parlor in his house. He knew he was ranting, but he couldn't seem to help it. He'd wanted to reach over and give Maddy a good shake.

He knew she cared for them more than she wanted to let on, but she didn't seem to know how to bridge the gap between self-sufficiency and self-confidence.

"I've never see you so manly and so pissed. Makes me hot."

Lucas stopped and spun around to look at Chase. The expression on the younger man's face was pure devilry. When he raised his eyebrows suggestively, Lucas gave in to the moment and chuckled. He walked over to Chase and hugged him.

"Hopefully the shock of our anger and exit will be the jolt Maddy needs," Chase said as he returned the hug. "If not, spanking is still an option."

"Hmm. Now that I think about it, that idea is getting *me* hot."

"Oh yeah? How hot? And hot to do? Or to get?"

In answer, Lucas took Chase's hand and placed it on the front of his pants. "Both."

Chase fairly purred, closing his fingers around the denim covered hardness in a way that never failed to arouse Lucas even more.

"I'm hot," he confessed to the younger man now. "I'm hot for you. I don't need any more time. I'm ready. I want to feel you inside me."

"*Luc.*" Chase gathered him in and placed a string of kisses on the side of his face, his neck. Then he took his hand, intertwined their fingers, and led him to the bedroom.

The window stood open just a bit, a soft late spring breeze just stirring the closed curtains. It occurred to Lucas that since Chase had returned, it felt as if a fresh breeze had swept out the staleness of his *life*. The world had become one brilliant new and exciting horizon after another to explore. He felt as if he'd gone through his whole life before now, just going through the motions, but not fully alive.

He was *alive* now, and didn't know if he could hold any more joy inside him. For the most part, he'd let Chase take the lead in setting the parameters to their relationship and in their lovemaking. When it came to the two of them, Chase was the man of experience, Lucas the eager if unsure virgin.

That would change tonight.

He remembered telling Chase that first time that he didn't know how—didn't know the rules or the etiquette or, quite frankly, the mechanics.

Tonight, his heart *showed* him how.

"No, let me," he said when Chase reached for the buttons of his shirt. With gentle motions, Lucas undressed them both. Each new bit of Chase's skin he uncovered, he stroked and kissed. With hands and lips and tongue he tried to tell this sexy younger man what he didn't have the words yet to say. He lavished attention on chest and arms, neck and navel. When he knew his own knees would buckle, he guided them to the bed.

Kisses slid from light and flirty to full open-mouthed splendor. Hot and wet and carnal, they stoked the flames of passion. Chest to chest, Lucas reveled in the feel of Chase's hard muscled body against his own. Their cocks brushed and danced, and the velvety heat of those silky touches nearly made Luc come. For long minutes they kissed and petted, allowing their bodies to brush and rub against each other. There burned such passion here, such emotion, that Lucas really felt as if this would be a first time in more than just the physical.

When Chase's arms wrapped around him, when his hands splayed over his back and across his ass, Lucas's pulse spiked.

"My turn." His lover whispered, and Lucas gladly surrendered. He turned onto his belly when urged, and groaned as Chase's tongue lapped and tasted the flesh of his shoulders, the small of his back. Over and over Chase's tongue paid tribute to Lucas's body and Lucas shivered in response. Chase nearly lay atop him and the heat from the younger man's body warmed him inside and out. Chase stroked him, neck to feet, lavishing attention on every inch of Lucas's skin. The caress of those strong masculine hands over the curve of his ass aroused him tremendously. Responding to the gentle prodding, he raised his buttocks, spread his legs.

Lucas shivered as Chase's fingers stroked over his opening, then down and around to tease and cup his scrotum. The slide of a drawer told Lucas that Chase would protect them both. Then he lost all thought as teeth sank gently into his ass, as hands reached around to stroke and glide over his cock. The strength of Chase's grip, the firm pumping action thrilled Lucas, sending his arousal even higher, so that all he wanted to do was wallow in it. His hips rocked, nature urging him to reach for more. Chase's gentle chuckle washed over him.

The moist heat of his lover's tongue stroking back and forth over his anus excited him, and he felt the rosebud flesh flex as if to grab more of the wonderful wetness.

"Please," he begged, knowing he could beg and be rewarded, knowing he was safe to beg or plead or demand. "Oh, please, Chase, *fuck* me."

"Here, now sweetheart. I'm going to give you what you need. I've wanted to be inside you for so long."

Lucas felt the bed dip, felt Chase move forward, then the hot, sheathed end of Chase's cock pressed against his rosebud, opening him.

"*Yes.*" Lucas had never wanted anything more than he wanted to feel the slick glide of that man flesh into his ass. He pushed back as Chase leaned into him. The pressure was more intense than when he'd taken the plugs, but also more erotic. This was his lover. The burning increased as his anal opening stretched. Hot, full, the latex covered shaft entered him inch by hot, hard inch. Lucas groaned, the sensation so intense, so wondrous, he only wanted more.

"Easy, lover. Let yourself stretch a bit more. You feel so sweet around me, but I don't want to hurt you. I never want to hurt you."

"I don't care. You can't hurt me, Chase. Please, give me more," Lucas begged, pushing back, flexing his inner ring.

"Lucas."

It thrilled him that he could make this young stud nearly lose control. Braced on hands and knees, he could only push back, invite Chase to take more.

"More, then."

Chase adjusted his position, and Lucas felt the heat of his body cover him. His lover trembled, and Lucas relished the power of their connection, that they would both shiver in need for each other. Lucas wanted everything this young man could give him. He pushed back and flexed.

Chase sank into him to the hilt.

"Hold still." Chase's voice strained as he fought to hang on to his control. Lucas didn't want his lover's restraint. He wanted his unfettered passion.

"Take more," Lucas urged.

"Sweetheart."

Lucas could almost hear the chains that had held Chase back snap. His lover pulled out nearly all the way then sank home again. The velvet cord of pain wrapped around the silken thread of lust, and

Lucas reveled in the whole of it. Long, strong strokes in a rhythm that sang of passion, need and greed became the center of the world for him. Pounding, driven thrusts shook the bed, and Lucas released the last tiny hold on his inhibitions, spreading himself wide open, ready to take everything his lover gave him.

"Yes. Oh Chase, *yes*." Lucas felt the stirring that told him he was on the verge of coming. When Chase reached around and stroked his cock again, Lucas cried out, his entire body rigid with rapture.

Chase's thrusts surged, his words laced in locked-jaw passion. "Yeah, take me. Take it all. Come with me."

The pounding orgasm shot out of him, long explosive streams of ecstasy that raced his heart and heated his blood. The spasms from Chase's cock buried deep within him filled his heart with joy. He and no one else had given his lover that pleasure. On and on it soared until, sated, Lucas collapsed on the bed.

Sweat bathed him, his lover covered him. The breeze wafted through the open window, kissing them both.

* * * *

He crept away from the house, away from the open window so they wouldn't hear him, wouldn't know he'd seen them.

The curtain had blocked most of the view, but not all of it. Even now, the sounds of their rutting echoed in his mind. The flash of naked skin moving, sliding had taunted him, the unnatural lure of it compelling him to watch even as he condemned.

Filthy faggots. How dare they bring their sickness here?

When he'd seen them on Maddy's porch the other day, he'd been repulsed. But then he'd had second thoughts. As he'd huddled down in his bed in the bunkhouse that night, he began to wonder if he'd really seen what he thought had. Maybe, just maybe, he'd been mistaken. He made himself think and think. Chase had grown up here, hadn't he? Maybe what he'd seen had been more in the way of father-son affection.

So he'd awakened and known that he had to be sure. He needed to know for certain if what he'd already witnessed was sickness, or if it had only been his imagination.

Now he had no doubts. They were queer boys, the two of them. Playing their sick sex games right here where he lived!

Did Maddy know? Did she suspect? He'd heard them yelling earlier, and he wondered if she'd somehow found out her foreman and the prodigal son were poking each other in the night.

She couldn't know. She wouldn't let them stay if she knew, would she? Far as he'd ever been able to tell, Maddy was decent folk.

Maybe he should tell her. Maybe he should march right up to the house and tell her right now.

Of course, likely they had her so fooled that she would never believe him.

Anger and hatred burned in him as he thought about what those two were doing even now in the foreman's bed. He pounded his fist into his hand, and imagined he pounded their faces instead.

He couldn't just stand back and let them carry on like this, doing unnatural things to each other. He couldn't just stand back and risk himself. What if one or the other of them came on to him? What if they both attacked him at the same time? Could he fight them both off? What if they grabbed him in the middle of the night?

Of course, he wasn't alone in the bunkhouse. He felt pretty sure the others would come to help him if he cried out. But maybe it would be a good idea to sleep with his gun close at hand. Just in case.

In the meantime, he couldn't just sit back and wait for them to make a move on him. How long until they got bored poking each other and wanted fresh meat? He knew how their kind operated. His father had warned him, hadn't he? They trolled the streets, the highways and the byways, looking for those they could con into serving as their whores. They'd pretend to be your friend, but in the end all they wanted was to stick their filthy dicks in you. Yes, he knew how these sick bastards lured the unsuspecting.

But he wouldn't be lured. He knew the truth now. And because he did, he couldn't let things be. He couldn't let them get away with this.

No, he would have to act. He would have to do something to make sure they got what they deserved. *Filthy faggots deserved to roast in the fires of Hell.*

Yes. That's what he'd do. He would make sure they roasted in Hell.

* * * *

Maddy had lain awake most of the night.

In the aftermath of their fight, on the heels of her tears, came a waspish anger she'd never known before. How *dare* they make her feel guilty for wanting to keep some things to herself? Did Chase and Luc think they could just snap their fingers and she would jump through hoops for them? Or did they figure that poor little female Maddy needed the big brave men and take care of her? Fight her battles for her? As if she was too vapid to take care of herself, fight for herself.

Well, so what if she didn't know what to do about Kevin just yet? She'd been doing for herself since she'd been a teenager, since her father's first stroke. If she'd waited for someone to take care of her back then, she'd still be waiting. Life had taught her that she had two strong arms to carry her own load; and in her hands, the ball would be far less likely to get dropped. Her mother had left when she'd been barely five, and in all the years since there had never been anyone she could trust to be there for her.

But then as the hours of the night had crept passed, she recalled how she'd felt, thinking that something had upset Lucas and Chase. And she remembered that fierce need—the need to take care of them, to fix whatever was wrong, because she loved them.

Wasn't that what Lucas had meant when he'd said that everything about her was their business? She had been ready to do battle to pull the secrets out of her lovers, to solve any problem, right any wrong. She wanted that, and yet had no doubt they could solve their own problems and fight their own battles. Wanting to do it for them, take care of them, didn't mean she wanted to diminish them. So then, how could she resent the same desire in them?

Did it mean they loved her? If they did, how could she love them and yet resent their loving her in return?

Now as dawn dusted the horizon, the depth of the chasm yawning between herself and her lovers seemed daunting. Lucas had said that she knew where she could find them when she figured it out. But as she began to feel the full weight of what her mulish pride had done to her relationship with both men, she wondered.

What if the chasm was too wide, too deep to breach? What if she'd already done too much damage to the relationship they'd been building together to mend the rift?

She still hadn't come up with a solution to her own pressing dilemma. No way in hell she would marry Kevin. Did she doubt he would carry through with his threat?

There was a chance he wouldn't, but she couldn't be sure. She'd known the little bastard most of her life. He was a worm, in every respect. Completely selfish, he owned not one scruple when it came to doing someone dirt if it could get him ahead. But did that mean he would stoop so low as to see her thrown in jail? What could he possibly benefit from that?

Spite. Yes, the little prick could and likely would feed her to the lions simply out of spite.

Maddy felt the stress of her sleepless night and Kevin's threat pushing down on her shoulders. She was tired. Truthfully, she felt far more exhausted than one sleepless night would allow.

Maybe Kevin wouldn't carry through with his threat. Maybe he would. But with each passing minute she realized that Kevin and his threat really weren't the biggest danger to her heart or her peace of mind. What she'd done to her relationship with her lovers by lying to them—even if that lie was one of omission—could cost her more than her ranch or her freedom.

It could cost her heart and her soul.

Maybe Lucas and Chase didn't love her. And maybe, just maybe, if she turned to them for help they would let her down the way that everyone she'd ever let close had let her down all her life. Maybe.

And maybe not.

Grabbing her jeans off the bedroom floor where she'd tossed them the night before, she pulled them on. Tucking her nightshirt into them, she worked her bare feet into her slippers and headed for the kitchen door.

She counted the steps she took rather than allowing her distrusting brain to do any more thinking.

The morning air chilled her arms. Rubbing them, she kept on walking until she'd reached the small stoop at the front of Lucas's house. The inner door had been opened a crack, and though it she could smell fresh coffee, hear the sound of quiet masculine conversation. She reached for the door handle then pulled back.

After the way she'd behaved last night, after what she'd kept hidden from them, she had no right to just intrude on them. She had no right to assume she would be welcome.

Screwing up her nerve, she knocked. It didn't take long for the inside door to be pulled open. She'd wondered which one of them would answer her summons. Somehow, she was unsurprised when they both did.

Neither man said anything, choosing instead to wait. To let her finish taking that first step. At least, please God, she hoped they were.

Did they have any idea the enormity of the chance she was about to take? Looking into first Luc's eyes, and then Chase's, she thought that maybe—just maybe—they did.

Maddy closed her eyes for one moment. Then she took a giant leap of faith.

"I'm in trouble. Serious trouble. And I don't know what to do about it. Please help me."

Chapter 11

"You look like hell, Maddy," Lucas said as he set a cup of coffee in front of her.

"Gee, thanks."

Chase chuckled. "You have a silver tongue, my love," he said to Lucas.

His hand caressed Maddy's head then he leaned down and gave her a quick kiss. When they'd heard the knock and seen her standing there, his first, somewhat cynical thought was that she'd come around awfully quickly. He'd wondered if she'd truly seen the light.

But when Lucas opened the door and pulled her into his arms, she'd burst into tears. And it occurred to Chase then that in all the years he'd known her, all those years he'd lived on the Circle D and followed her around like a faithful lap dog, he'd never once seen her cry. He'd been pissed because Maddy had refused to confide in them. Now he thought he could see the bigger picture. Her reticence really had nothing to do with either himself or Lucas. She was the way she was because she'd had to be, she'd had to protect herself over the years. He also understood that she'd been solitary in a very basic way for far too long.

Solitary could be a very hard habit to break.

"Hush now, darlin', hush. Whatever it is, we'll fix it," Lucas had crooned. The depth of the older man's feelings for Maddy matched what Chase knew to be his feelings for himself. Lucas may not say much, but his emotions ran true and deep.

Now as Chase sat on Maddy's left side, he took her hand in his and brought it to his lips. Lucas sat on her right, a hand on her back, rubbing gently.

"Why don't you start by telling us about that photograph?" Chase asked quietly. "You bought drugs?"

Maddy nodded her head, and took a moment to wipe her eyes on the hankie Lucas had given her.

"I'm not sure when it was taken. It could have been at any time during the last six months of dad's life."

"Go on," Lucas urged.

Maddy took a sip from her coffee, then set it down and rubbed both palms on her jeans. "You remember, Lucas, how sick Dad got that last year?"

"I do."

She turned to Chase. "The strokes he'd suffered in the last couple of years had left him…changed. Surly and difficult. He couldn't get around that well, which made everything worse. And he was in so much pain." She paused now, let her gaze wander out the kitchen window. Chase wondered if she envisioned those days, seeing again the deterioration of her only parent.

"I'd asked Doctor Albertson—Doc Morton in Marshville had passed on Dad's care to him over in Colorado Springs—anyway, I'd asked the Doctor to prescribe stronger pain medication for dad, but he didn't believe in managing pain that way. He thought Dad should be taken to pain management classes, so that he could learn how to live with 'the discomfort'."

"What was this guy, a fucking moron?" Chase couldn't keep the anger out of his tone. He felt pissed for both Maddy and her father. No one should have to suffer through such pain when medication was available and could help. Plus, he could well imagine how hard living with Robert Dalton had become for Maddy in that last half year. Yeah, the man had treated Chase pretty well, but he'd never been overly pleasant in is treatment of his daughter, and Chase had been aware of that.

"He just didn't understand, and Doc Morton wasn't about to step on his colleague's toes."

"So you went out and got what he needed off the street?"

"I had to. I didn't think I had any choice. It took me a while to find someone who could help. I finally met someone who knew someone who could get me pain meds for dad without a prescription."

"Damn it, Maddy!"

"I'm sorry Chase, I know it was illegal but—"

"Screw illegal. I don't give a flying fuck about *illegal*. What you did was dangerous. Damn it all to hell, sweetheart, people who deal drugs aren't the safest people to be around."

"It's not like the guy was selling cocaine or acid. I bought morphine, and some other pain killers. But mostly morphine."

The look on her face, innocent bewilderment, just made Chase's blood run cold with fear. *My God, the woman hadn't even realized what she'd been doing.*

Lucas must have come to the same conclusion. "Maddy, the guy wasn't selling *you* cocaine or acid. But he *was* a drug dealer—you can bet he had a whole menu of illegal substances. And likely was a very dangerous man."

"Oh."

"Yeah, 'oh'." Just the thought that something seriously bad could have happened to Maddy and he'd have been unable to do anything about it—hell he wouldn't have even known about it because he'd been dragging his ass coming home—made Chase close his eyes for a long moment. He'd brushed up against the world inhabited by those who had little regard for human dignity or human life, those who had no scruples and no compunction against hurting innocents. He knew what could happen to the ill-prepared and the unsuspecting in this world. Knowing how close Maddy had really come to being another statistic made him want to puke.

"That's done," Lucas said in his quiet, no-nonsense way. "And, fortunately, you came through that without becoming another victim."

His gaze met Lucas's. It shouldn't surprise him that Lucas, who claimed not to be able to read people well, could read him. Knowing he could was a wonderful, comforting feeling.

Because he needed the contact, he reached out and stroked Maddy's head. "There's still the photograph," Chase said. "Who sent it to you?"

"Kevin Marsh brought it the other day."

Chase had to hang on to his temper with both hands as Maddy told them about Marsh's visit the day he and Lucas had gone into Gunnison.

"He's given me until Sunday. I either agree to marry him and turn this ranch over to him, or he sends that photograph to Attorney-General Beecham. Maybe you don't know, because you've been out of the state, but this guy is building a solid reputation of being a hard-ass about cracking down on the drug culture in Colorado. His news conferences have been all over the television the last few months. My, um, dealer actually is in prison right now as a result of a state-wide sting operation that Beecham spear-headed. Well, according to Marsh he is, at any rate."

"I've a good mind to drive into town and break that little prick's fucking legs." Lucas sounded even angrier than he had been the night before.

"If I thought it would be any kind of real solution, I'd help you." Chase sent a smile of commiseration over to the other man.

"What am I going to do? It's Thursday already. Sunday is coming up pretty damn fast."

"You're sure as hell *not* going to marry Kevin Marsh or turn this ranch over to him." Lucas's tone brooked no argument, not that Chase thought Maddy would give him one.

"Of course not," she agreed quickly. "But you *know* him. He'll probably make good on his threat. What am I going to do?"

She looked on the verge of breaking down again. "What you are going to do is trust us," Chase said quietly. "Right now, you're beat. Did you get any sleep at all last night?" Lucas had been right, she *did* look like hell.

"No. I was too upset. I'm sorry. I...I didn't mean to hurt you guys."

"Hush, baby. Don't worry about that. Now the first order of business is for you get some rest. Lucas, maybe you could take Maddy back to her place and take care of her?" He only had to meet Lucas's gaze for a moment for the other man to understand his meaning. Chase half expected Maddy to bitch at him again for referring to her in the third person with her sitting right there. And didn't know what to think when she just sat there looking...lost.

"Maddy?"

When she turned her attention to him, he leaned over and kissed her again. "I'm going to make some phone calls, see if I can get us a clearer picture of the situation, and what our options might be. Then later, after you've slept, we'll have a look at what we've got, and see if we can come up with a good plan. Nothing happens unless you approve. All right?"

"Yes, all right."

He could see by the look on her face that wasn't what she'd expected to have happen at all. Clearly she'd believed that he and Lucas would simply steam-roll over her. Maddy was operating under a lot of misconceptions.

First they'd deal with Mister Sleaze. *Then* they'd work on the rest of those misconceptions.

* * * *

Kevin stared down at the message slip his secretary had left on his desk before taking her worthless ass off to lunch. Barnes wanted him to call, and he'd had Maebelle mark the message 'urgent'.

He swallowed hard, then crumpled the slip and tossed it into the trash. He could say he never got the message. Yes, that's what he'd do. He'd even fire the bitch to back up his claim.

But Barnes would still expect to hear from him. He couldn't go around forever with his cell phone turned off, dodging messages. For one, he was an important man, everybody in Marshville knew that. Important men always got calls on their cell phones, wherever they went. If he'd only thought ahead and paid extra for it, he could have had the service that would have allowed him to have Barnes' number blocked. Maybe he'd look into that. Important men controlled who had access to them.

Kevin hunched his shoulders, trying to slide away from the tension. He shouldn't have given Maddy so much time to make her decision. *Should have gotten her in the house, alone, is what I should have done. Those two assholes from last Saturday hadn't been in sight. I should have taken advantage of their absence, gotten her inside the house. Then I could have persuaded her.* One thing he knew for certain. The moment he had a ring on her finger, he would show her the proper way for a woman to behave. And he'd throw in a few rounds with his belt as payment for the trouble she'd given him so far.

He had no doubt she would be his wife, and in short order, too. A woman without male kin, she had no choice but to accept his offer. What else *could* she do? She sure as hell wouldn't deny him. Not at the price of her freedom.

In the meantime, he only had to avoid speaking to Barnes for another few days. How hard could *that* be?

The phone rang, and Kevin just stared at it. Telling himself he wasn't afraid, he just shouldn't be lowering himself to answering his own phone, he scooped his hat off the credenza behind him, and headed out.

Lunch time was a busy time in town. He'd take a drive down Main Street, let everyone see him. Maybe he'd stop by the florist, pick up whatever posies they had on sale and take them out to his Aunt Verna.

The only flowers he really wanted to buy that old bitch would be for her coffin. His Aunt Verna held tightly to the purse strings these days, which was the reason Kevin had decided to sell his land—well, his and Maddy's—to Barnes Developments in the first place.

Why his father had to up and leave most of the family assets under the control of his dried up old prune of a sister, Kevin would never understand. He could only be grateful that both his Auntie and the lawyer who managed the accounts had such taciturn personalities. Everyone thought *he* raked in the profits from the seed and feed, and from his real estate business. It wasn't general knowledge that Kevin had been left dependent on his Aunt for a salary in return for actually overseeing the family businesses.

Kevin had nearly resigned himself to his dismal fate until late last year. Rick Barnes, a land developer from New York City, had visited the area looking for land suitable to build a resort. Kevin's mother's uncle had left him what had at one time been the family ranch, land adjacent to the Dalton spread. At the time of his inheritance, Kevin had been pissed. What the hell was he supposed to do with a small parcel of land? The ranch house was tiny, in disrepair. The barn wasn't much better. Uncle Crawford had sold off what stock he'd had years before. When the old boy had croaked, the land had passed to Kevin. *Like he was ever going to be a rancher.*

Not in this life.

Kevin knew the value of the small spread, and it wasn't much. Neither of the ranchers on either side of the place—the Daltons or the Comstocks—had shown any interest in buying the place.

But when Rick Barnes had wandered into his real estate office last year, asking about available properties, it had started Kevin thinking.

The amount of acreage Barnes wanted surpassed the pissant spread his uncle had left him; but if he added in the Dalton place, especially when he considered the stream that ran through both places, and that hot spring of Maddy's—why, then he had something worth offering the developer.

So a deal had been struck, Kevin had received that hefty down payment, and there remained just one tiny detail left to be seen to.

Kevin had to get his hands on Maddy Dalton's ranch.

The only way he'd thought of to do that was to marry the bitch. Not that he would mind, necessarily. He figured an ignorant country bimbo like her would be grateful someone offered for her. He wouldn't mind fucking her, really. And she'd been so damn high and mighty with him—just like that old broad Verna—he'd enjoy giving her the discipline she needed. She'd learn her place if he had anything to say about it.

Funny, but Barnes hadn't batted an eye when he'd discovered Kevin had negotiated the deal behind Maddy's back. He didn't seem to care how he got the land, just as long as he got it.

Clouds had blown in since that morning, and the day had turned overcast. Kevin got into his car, taking the time to put the windows up. *Wouldn't do to get rain in the Caddy.*

Yes, he'd buy flowers for Aunt Verna and tell her that there were nuptials on the horizon. The old bitch would likely be beside herself with joy. How often did she nag him about getting married? Just about every chance she got. If he knew Verna, she'd approve of Maddy, too. One stone cold bossy bitch would certainly appreciate another.

He'd tell the old biddy that he and his newly betrothed would come by for a visit Sunday evening. A smile split his face as he realized that he could likely get the old bat to give him a few thousand dollars if he hinted at the fact he didn't yet have a ring.

Women, Kevin Marsh groused as he headed his Caddy toward the florist shop at the other end of town, were simple creatures. He'd sweet talk the old one, discipline the young one, and soon his life would be damn near perfect.

Chapter 12

There had been many times in the past when Maddy seemed stressed, when she'd looked like what she needed more than anything else in the world was some old fashioned tender loving care. During those times, Lucas had cursed himself for a coward, too afraid to step up and take care of her the way he longed to. He'd been too afraid that once he built a relationship with her, she would somehow sense the secret desire locked deep inside him—the desire for man flesh—and be repulsed by him, turn him away.

What a miracle that he could step in now, take care of her, and follow his heart.

Lucas closed the door behind them and steered Maddy into one of the kitchen chairs. "I'm going to run a hot bath for you, sweetheart."

"You don't have to," she replied quietly. "Now that I've told you guys what's been weighing me down, now that I know you don't hate me, I'll be fine. I *do* feel better. Knowing that you're going to help me, that I'm not alone…it's better. I'm just so tired. I just need to sleep."

Lucas crouched in front of her. "Would you spoil my fun? I've wanted to pamper you, it seems like forever. Likely some day in the future, I'll need you to pamper me. But today, this is my turn to have a small dream of mine come true. Would you deny me that?"

Maddy's eyes unexpectedly filled with tears, and one drop overflowed, the track down her cheek glistening. "I'm really an ungrateful bitch, aren't I? I don't mean to be."

"Shh. You're not." It tore Lucas's heart to see her like this. But the way he had it figured, she'd been long overdue to let things go. He didn't know a lot about women, but he did know they were built differently than men, on the inside. Men seemed to have an easier time soldiering on without breaking down; not that men didn't feel emotions every bit as deeply as women. They just seemed better suited to suppressing life's bumps and bruises and pains. Women, on the other hand, seemed to need the cleansing balm of tears. Maddy had held hers back so long, she'd probably need longer to get them all out.

He kissed her and then headed for the bathroom. Rooting around, he couldn't find any of the fussy stuff women sometimes added to their baths for ritual or for comfort. So he ran a tub of very warm water and added a generous dollop of shampoo.

Lucas returned to the kitchen, his heart squeezing a little when he saw Maddy sitting exactly as he'd left her. That was a measure of her exhaustion. He stopped in front of her and gently helped her to her feet.

"Come on."

When they were in the bathroom, he undressed her and helped her into the tub.

"You lie back and let me take care of you. Okay?"

"You're going to bathe me? Are you going to tuck me in, too?"

"Eventually," he replied.

"No one's ever done that for me."

He had the soap and cloth in hand when those words, whispered, nailed him hard in the gut. Everyone deserved to be coddled from time to time. He was looking forward to when it would be his turn. For the moment, though, he focused his attention on Maddy.

"My good fortune, then, that I get to be the first. Now just lay back and relax."

"You touching me all over isn't exactly going to make me relax."

Lucas chuckled, pleased to see the spark of humor in her eyes. "Oh, I promise you that it will, eventually."

* * * *

Maddy shivered in response to the unbelievably soft brush of soapy cloth against her breasts. The expression on Lucas' face as he slowly bathed her was one of absolute absorption. Never before had she been the center of someone's attention this way. Her confession to her lovers and the decision she'd made to let someone else be in control for a while, coupled with them wanting to care for her eased her heart. Warm water soothed her muscles; fragrant bubbles soothed her senses; but Lucas' delicious touch subtly lit the fire of her arousal.

"Close your eyes, darlin'. Just feel what I'm doing to you. Let this be the only thing in your world."

She easily complied with the request. Easy, because doing so brought such pleasure. Everywhere he touched came alive with a sultry, satiny need for him. Whenever he'd touched her since that first time, she'd sensed a singular, fierce focus in him. Chase, as a lover, was energetic and playful. Lucas was reverent.

No one had ever given her this kind of attention, this kind of care. He touched and bathed and caressed as if the only thing he wanted in the entire world was to make her feel good. The last of her tension evaporated, and with it the darkness that had always been trapped in the depths of her soul.

"Open your legs for me, Maddy."

Oh, God. Lucas' fingers trailed the edge of the cloth, finding and teasing her clit until she writhed with need. Cupping his hands, he scooped water over her to rinse her. Bending over the edge of the tub, he captured her lips with his own.

Maddy lost herself to the passion of his kiss. His tongue tasted her, drank her, and she responded with all she had. He'd wooed her completely when she hadn't even realized she'd needed, so desperately, to be wooed.

"Mind your feet." Reaching out he turned on the faucet, putting more hot water into the tub. "You soak for just a couple of minutes longer, and I'll be right back."

Maddy thought she might have dozed, because it seemed only seconds passed before Lucas returned, carrying a bundle of towels.

He helped her to stand then wrapped her in the towels he must have heated in the dryer. Though it was nearly summer, exhaustion had left her feeling a little chilled and shaky. Being wrapped in warmed towels was the most luxurious sensation she'd ever experienced. When he scooped her into his arms and carried her to her bed, she laid her head on his shoulder and enjoyed the sensation of being treasured.

She lifted her arms when he asked so he could dry her, and when he laid her on the bed and whispered for her to roll over onto her tummy, she complied.

She heard the sound of his clothes hitting the floor, and thought she knew what would come next, but she was mistaken.

He straddled her, the flesh of his lean strong thighs hot against her skin. She could feel his cock, already rigid and his scrotum, hot and tight with his seed as they rested against her buttocks and she wanted to maneuver so she could feel them against her feminine folds. She'd already become wet for him and wanted him.

He had other plans.

The sudden sensation of warm liquid dropping onto her back startled her. Then his hands began smoothing, caressing, massaging.

"Oh, *yes*. Mmm." Speech eluded her as he worked magic on her flesh, his fingers digging in slightly to relax her muscles yet stir her juices. She'd never had a back rub, never understood the allure in it. Now she did.

"If you stop I'll murder you."

Lucas's laugh, sounding so deep and smug, fluttered her belly and curled her toes. "I promise I won't stop until you're so satisfied, you drop into sleep."

He worked at totally pampering her body until she believed she *would* sleep. And then, gently, subtly, he began to arouse her. Small touches along the sides of her breasts, down her legs then up on the inside of her thighs. Tiny nips of teeth on her ass, the play of his tongue on the small of her back or against the shell of her ear.

Soon she was whimpering, her hips rising as if to receive his penis deep into her body. She heard the sound of him protecting them both, and her heart beat faster. His hands urged her to raise her bottom. His latex covered cock, hot and hard, brushed against the excited flesh of her ass then slid down until it rubbed seductively between the lips of her pussy.

"Please."

"Please what, Maddy?"

"Please...fuck me. *Lucas*!"

He'd thrust into her before she finished begging, burying himself deep in one bold stroke, holding himself deep as he leaned forward. His hot moist breath bathed her ear as he sucked her earlobe into his mouth. He wasn't thrusting in and out, it felt more like he swiveled his hips in a slow, tight circle. He was going to drive her insane. She would die from sexual need right here in her own bed.

"Can you use your pussy muscles to squeeze my cock, baby? Squeeze and release...ah, yeah, just like that. Keep squeezing and releasing."

He began to pump into her, long slow and deep thrusts so that her inner muscles grasped at a cock that kept surging and retreating, surging and retreating. One masculine hand pushed under her until it held a breast.

When Lucas began to pinch and pull her nipple in the same cadence as his cock moved in and out of her, Maddy cried out, her orgasm a tsunami that flooded her. On and on it came as Lucas thrust harder and deeper. The slap of his balls on her ass echoed with her whimpering cries as wave after wave of rapture continued to crash through her. Then Lucas's grunts joined in as his cock began to pulse inside her, filling the condom with a hot ejaculation that she could feel against her cervix despite the latex covering it.

The end of his cock hit something just inside her tunnel on his next thrust and her orgasm erupted anew, this explosion so sharp and unexpected, she screamed.

Maddy sighed. Lucas covered her like a warm blanket, pressing her into the mattress, the music of their labored breathing the only sound in the room. She couldn't move, she couldn't speak, and didn't want to. When he lifted off her, she mewed. When he pulled the blankets out from under her she thought she might have whimpered, but couldn't be sure. Then the bed dipped, and he slid in beside her, his naked flesh hot against hers. Safe, protected, she slid into a deep and dreamless sleep.

* * * *

Lucas opened his eyes, instantly awake. He'd not meant to fall asleep so much as to simply hold his woman while *she* slept. She'd curled into him and the warmth of her naked breasts against his chest gave him a singular satisfaction.

He guessed he was an unusual man, because he was in love—totally, absolutely and completely in love—with two people at the same time. This had to be the most wonderful feeling in the world, and the most frightening. He'd never had anything to lose before, and now he did. Of course, he'd never really had a reason to live before, either, and now he did.

He'd let his worry escape when he and Chase had been alone in Gunnison. How amazing that Chase had understood his fears even before he'd fully understood them, himself.

Lucas didn't want this—whatever it was the three of them had together—to be only a short term thing. He didn't want it only to be for the moment. He wanted it to last.

He wanted forever.

Beside him, Maddy began to stir. He set his worries away and gathered her closer. He placed a kiss on her head, and waited to see if she would settle again.

"What time is it?" her sleep-husky voice stroked over his skin.

He had to stretch to see the clock. "Nearly three. You've only slept for about four hours."

"Feels longer."

Sound had them both looking toward the doorway. Chase stood, hands on his hips, smile on his face.

"Don't you two look cozy?" he asked.

"We are. You should join us," Maddy invited.

"Don't mind if I do. And I wonder if this is the right time to ask you for a favor?"

Maddy chuckled, and Lucas couldn't help thinking the laugh sounded lighter than he'd ever heard it.

"Well if you can't ask a favor when you're naked and in bed with your lovers, when can you?"

"There you go."

Lucas thoroughly enjoyed watching Chase undress. He was one hell of a sexy package. The sight of his cock, fully erect, stirred Lucas's libido. He shifted slightly. Maddy had turned over as Chase had approached the side of the bed, and now Lucas pulled her closer to make room for the other man. She obviously felt his erection and nestled her ass against him.

"Are you going to ask that favor?" Her voice betrayed her own renewed arousal, and Lucas knew the afternoon delights weren't quite finished for the day.

"Yeah, now that I'm naked and in bed with you both, I am. I want to buy a king sized bed and have it set up in here. I want us to have more room to play in. What do you say? Will you let me do that for us?"

Lucas doubted the significance of the question escaped Maddy. Chase's offer was a gift, and a promise at the same time. He hadn't told her, he'd asked.

"Yes. I think we need a bigger bed. Then we can all spend the night together. So, yes, I'll accept your offer. Thank you."

"You're welcome. Now I have one more favor to ask."

Lucas recognized the look in Chase's eyes. He felt his dick harden even more as the other man held up a condom package. Not saying a word, he tore it open with his teeth then sheathed his fully erect cock.

Lucas reached down and lifted Maddy's right leg over his hip, opening her. Chase moved between her thighs and thrust into her.

"*Chase.*" Maddy sighed his name and closed her eyes, obviously enjoying the other man's attentions as he began to pump himself into her. There was nothing tentative about the way Chase took her.

When Lucas met his eyes, he saw a determination that told him he could expect the same kind of feral mating.

"All afternoon I've been imagining what the two of you were doing over here naked and all over each other. Picturing you both fucking got me hot and hard. I decided that the only one thing for me to do was to come over and fuck you both brainless."

Lucas looked down over Maddy's shoulder, watched as one lover's latex-covered cock moved in and out of his other lover's eager pussy. Her breasts had plumped, her nipples beaded, and Lucas helped himself, rolling the rock hard pebbles between thumb and forefinger. Then he looked up and encountered Chase's heated gaze.

Leaning forward, Luc kissed him, his tongue going deep in Chase's mouth, drinking him in with unrestrained passion. When Chase eased back, bent down to take Maddy's nipple in his mouth, Maddy stretched her neck back, offering Lucas her own lips. Lucas kissed her with the same heat, the same love.

Chase's hand reached around Maddy's ass, his fingers closed around Luc's cock, and then he felt Maddy's hand there too. Lucas weaned his lips from Maddy's, his gaze going from one to the other of his lovers.

Lucas's emotions overflowed. "Yes, Chase. Fuck us both. Take us both. We belong to you."

"Do you?" Chase asked, the rocking of his hips in perfect sync with the milking motion of his hand on Lucas' cock. "Maddy, do you?" A ferocity had come into Chase's eyes, and an intensity that Lucas hadn't seen before. But he'd known it existed, had sensed its presence and had yearned to see it, feel it. In his heart, Lucas had known and loved the dominant in Chase and now that he saw it, felt eager to submit. He rocked his hips so that he could offer his lover more of his cock, spread his woman's legs slightly wider so he could offer his lover more of her pussy, knowing, *knowing* in that moment that they *were* all one, and that he did belong to Chase, totally and completely.

He rested his head on top of Maddy's, doing what he could to push her into Chase, silently urging her to submit, too.

"Yes…yes…I belong to you," her cry erupted out of the heart of her, the most beautiful sound in the world. "Oh, God, Chase, *harder*."

Lucas began to come, his hiss of completion just a heart beat ahead of both his lovers'. And the words Chase whispered then sounded like a vow and sent him higher.

"We belong to each other."

Chapter 13

"I have some contacts, so I made a few phone calls." Chase waited until the coffee had been brewed and the three of them dressed and sitting at the kitchen table before broaching the subject on everyone's mind.

"A good friend of mine, Philip Haggerty, is a lawyer with his own investigation agency and ties to the Justice Department." He decided not to risk any needless pissy feelings by mentioning he'd already asked Phil to take a look at Marsh. He could see no need to let Maddy know he'd been planning to help her whether she had wanted him to or not. "Outside of Justice, he has contacts all over—including, as it turns out, a lawyer with the attorney general's office in Denver. This man is a good friend of his. I gave Phil all the details I had and asked him to contact Sean Paris on our behalf."

"Isn't that...isn't that just doing what Marsh threatened to do in the first place?"

Chase recognized the fear on Maddy's face. He hated to be the one to have put it there, but there really was no easy or guaranteed way to get out of this mess.

"It's a risk, yes. I know you're scared. Trust me, so am I."

"You're scared?" Doubt laced her words. "You're not the one whose ass is on the line." Maddy's grumbling nearly made him smile. He didn't think she'd appreciate hearing how cute she seemed to him when she got that pouty, grumpy look on her face. He also wanted her to understand that she wasn't as alone as she thought.

"Maddy." Luc's soft rebuke got her attention, and she flushed.

"If you think for one minute that Luc and I aren't just as worried about what comes next as you are, then you don't understand how much you mean to us. I'm going to do everything in my power to help you stomp on Marsh's shit-eating face. And I know Luc feels the same way."

"Damn straight. Did your friend—Philip—have any kind of an idea what might happen? What we can expect?" Lucas asked.

"Well for one, the photograph by itself won't get Maddy into hot water. Yeah, it looks incriminating. But there aren't any details as to location, or time of day or even date. Also, without any sort of legal documentation to support it, there's no way anyone can even pin down how it was taken, or even what it's a photograph of."

"Oh. You mean…because it was taken by another drug dealer? That's what Marsh claimed." Hope had begun to blossom on Maddy's face. Chase regretted that he couldn't leave it at that. He *wanted* to leave it at that. But one of the things Maddy feared, deep in her heart, was that if she committed herself to a forever relationship, she'd lose control of her life. So as much as he longed to just tell her everything would be all right, he couldn't. She deserved to know the truth, and he deserved for her to know that he respected her right to have it.

"The value of a surveillance photo lies not just in the visual it provides, but in the documentation of the officers of the law who took it. They can testify where and when. This photo, by itself, isn't really evidence of anything. The danger to you lies in whether or not the other person pictured—your friendly neighborhood morphine supplier—can be coerced into testifying against you."

"You sound as if you know quite a lot about this sort of thing," Lucas said.

Trust Luc to zero in on that. "I do."

"Because of your friend, the lawyer?"

Well, hell, now Maddy had picked up on the scent. He heard enough doubt in her tone to tell him that. He could actually feel himself begin to blush. "Not exactly," he replied.

When the two of them just kept looking at him, he shrugged. *No big deal. I can be honest.* He wanted to be honest, come to that.

"I was fairly successful as a venture capitalist on Wall Street, and as a result, a few years ago, I was approached by an agent of the Treasury Department and asked to assist in an investigation. It involved a quick crash course in evidence gathering, police procedure, stuff like that."

"An agent of the Treasury Department? Did I know the Treasury Department had agents?" Maddy asked out loud.

"Sure you did," Lucas sent Chase a wink, "you know, ATF, DEA, Secret Service. Those are Treasury agents."

Maddy had given her attention to Lucas while he explained, but now she pinned Chase with her gaze. "You worked for the Secret Service?"

"It's not as glamorous as you might think. I assisted in a Secret Service investigation into a case of computer fraud based on the finessing of bank and stock securities. Treasury needed someone with a certain specialized knowledge and reputation for one particular type of case, that's all. The assignment lasted a few months, and ended successfully. After, I helped out on a few more cases before I decided law enforcement wasn't a career I wanted to pursue long term. While working with them, I met a lot of people. Philip, with whom I had a previous relationship, had been involved with Treasury at the time. In fact I've long suspected he was the reason I got tagged by the agency in the first place."

Maddy remained quiet for a long moment. "Can I even really afford to pay you what you're worth? Venture capitalist, knowledge and reputation…you're not exactly in need of the pay check I'm providing, are you? In fact, it probably seems like petty cash to you."

She was getting all righteous on him, allowing her ego be insulted because of some wild hare she'd just gotten that he might be slumming. Oh yes, if anybody wanted to give him a test on *Maddy*, he could pass it with flying colors, proving he knew her pretty well.

"Knock it off, Maddy," he said lightly. Picking up her hand he squeezed it, meeting her gaze, and then Luc's. "I'm not here for a pay check. I'm here because the two of you are here. This is home."

It was the closest Chase had come to declaring his love and he waited to see what the two people who meant the most to him in the world would do with the armor-plated heart he'd just handed them.

Lucas swallowed hard, and his eyes glistened. Maddy's breath hitched, and he could tell she was striving to hang on to her casual cool.

"Bet your ass you can buy that king sized bed. I have half a mind to make you spring for a hot tub, too. Always wanted a hot tub."

Her face turned a bright pink. Chase couldn't help it, he roared with laughter. "Yeah, a hot tub has amazing possibilities. We'll negotiate."

* * * *

"Wondered if you all were going to show up for dinner or not. What the hell am I over here cooking for if no one comes to eat?"

The uncharacteristic surly comment hit Maddy as soon as she entered the bunkhouse, Lucas and Chase in tow. Bill had his moments, but he wasn't usually that brusque. There'd been several times over the last year when she skipped the evening meal with the crew, when Lucas had as well. Still, she didn't want anyone on her staff being pissed with her if a few conciliatory words could avoid it.

"Sorry, Bill. There've been...issues the last few days that we've had to deal with."

"Food's ready."

Both Charlie and Pat seemed a bit uncomfortable in the silence that followed. Ralph Meade, the visiting horse handler from the K-Temple ranch made it to the table just as Maddy sat.

"Sorry I'm late, folks. Shadow needed a little extra attention. He can be high strung at times."

"You're not late," Maddy said. "We only just got here ourselves."

Bill seemed to perk up with the appearance of the guest. As the platter of pork chops and the bowls of mashed potatoes, gravy and vegetables got passed around the table, conversation picked up. Rather than contribute right away, Maddy decided to sit back and just listen. Had Bill been in a rotten mood for some reason that she needed to know about? Or had it been just one of those things?

The look on Pat and Charlie's faces told her that likely the older man had bitched some when she hadn't shown up for meals the last few days. Well, she guessed she couldn't really hold that against him. He always made sure a hot meal hit the table at the end of the day, and that wasn't a job Maddy ever wanted to have to take on herself. She'd rather be out in the hot sun digging post holes than in a hot kitchen cooking.

Before long, it seemed everyone had relaxed back into the usual camaraderie of dinner. This was the time of day she liked most generally, for it allowed her to touch base with her people, the one time of day when everyone came together like a family.

"I had a call late yesterday from Jordan Comstock," Maddy announced now. In fact, her neighbor's call had completely slipped her mind in the wake of more personal considerations. She tried not to think of what some of those considerations consisted of. She especially needed to keep this afternoon's activities off her mind. Her staff would wonder if she started blushing all over the damn place.

"Comstock says there have been reports of a cougar being spotted on the outskirts of Marshville. Have any of you men seen any cat signs near the herds?"

"I haven't noticed anything," Charlie said, "And that's something I always keep an eye out for. I once had a run in with a mad-as-hell mamma cat when I worked over the other side of Colorado Springs. Spooked the damn horse, dumped me on the ground. It was a close one, and not something I'd care to have happen again."

"Those cats can be mean bitches," Lucas agreed, "especially if they have young. Keep an eye out for tracks, or signs of a den. Let us know if you see anything at all."

"It's my preference to call in the wildlife people and have any cats removed rather than killed," Maddy said as she cut into her pork chop. "We can only do that if we see them before they threaten us."

"We'll keep our eyes open," Pat said. "Maybe we'll take a bit of extra time scouting around likely locales tomorrow, just to be sure."

"Good idea, thanks. Of course, if a situation arises, protect yourselves first."

"Don't worry, boss. We will."

Lucas picked up the rhythm of the conversation, asking questions of Pat and Charlie who been sent to monitor the livestock.

For the first time, Maddy fully realized how they'd always done this, been a team in running the ranch.

Her mind wandered, and she didn't realize she'd begun to play with her food. Maybe she'd never been as alone as she'd thought. Yeah, she'd felt the weight of responsibility early on, but a lot of that really had to do with her father and the way he'd treated her, the way he'd never seemed to be happy with anything she did.

But right from the beginning, Lucas had been there. In the background for the most part, but at her side when it counted. She shuddered just thinking how much more difficult the last few years would have been without him.

Now she had someone on her other side, too, someone she believed she would come to rely on just as much.

She'd been wrong when she'd told herself that she'd never been able to count on anyone. She'd always had Lucas.

"Bill, you figure we're about ready to have Selestial and Moon Dancer serviced? I bet Ralph here is eager to get home."

Lucas's question cut into her thoughts, and Maddy brought her attention back to the table.

"Aw, it's not so bad here." Ralph smiled as he made that comment.

Bill looked up from his plate. "Reckon day after tomorrow Moon Dancer will be prime. Maybe another day for Selestial."

Maddy raised one eyebrow. There'd been a chill in his response. Something had to be really bothering Bill for him to talk to Lucas that way. However, she didn't have the energy to tackle it right at the moment. So when Luc looked over at her, one eyebrow raised, she just shrugged and shook her head in the negative.

The exhaustion that had been relieved for a time that afternoon chose that moment to return full force, and it was all Maddy could do to finish her dinner. She'd had a few hours sleep that afternoon, and some of the best pampering and orgasms she could ever remember. Hell, the latter could be said of damn near every day since she'd taken on two lovers. But the last couple of days had taken it out of her, emotionally. Who could have guessed that keeping a secret from the ones who cared about you, even when you'd convinced yourself you were perfectly justified in doing so, could be so much effort and cause so much stress?

The chatter around the table carried on, but Maddy mostly listened. She also paid attention to Bill, and wondered why he kept shooting nasty looks at Chase. As she continued to just observe everyone and everything, she noticed Charlie give Chase some strange looks, too.

Hell, I'm just being paranoid.

"I think I'm going to call it a night." She'd eaten most of her dinner but had no desire for any dessert. Pushing away from the table, she got to her feet.

"If you're turning in, I'll come up to the house right now and finish working on your computer. It'll only take a few minutes then you can use it in the morning, first thing." Chase spoke as he got to his feet.

"Ah, sure. That would be great." Maddy said smoothly, despite the fact that Chase had just thrown her a curve. He hadn't been working on her computer at all.

To Lucas Chase said, "Snag me some cake, please. I'll be right back."

Everyone in the bunkhouse wished her a good night. One look in Chase's eyes as he held the door for her and she knew for certain that it was going to be a very good night indeed.

* * * *

He got away from everyone else as soon as he could. He didn't want them to see his anger. No, not anger. He'd gone beyond angry, bordering on furious.

He didn't like the way those two gay boys took all of Maddy's time and attention. Playing on her gentle heart, while the whole time they carried on with their sick sex games in the dark of night. He didn't want to see them anywhere *near* her. She was good and pure. They would taint her.

Maddy hadn't looked well tonight. As a matter of fact, he didn't think she'd been looking very healthy in the last few days at all. And in the last few days, every time he looked, there those two had been with her. Following her everywhere, crowding her out even in her own house.

Could just being near the two of them be making her sick? Who knew what all manner of disease and germs they carried around with them? He'd heard stories about the contamination gays carried and spread. He'd been on guard each night, only sleeping lightly, awakening at the smallest sound. No way one of those homos was going to crawl up his ass in the middle of the night. He slept with a gun under his pillow, and he'd taken to washing his hands with soap and hot water several times a day. Those were the only ways he could think of to protect himself.

No, that wasn't true. He knew of one other way he could protect himself—one way he could protect them all. He knew what to do to destroy the plague running rampant on the Circle D. He'd handle it the same way all plagues had been handled, down through the ages. He'd take the next day or so to be sure he had everything he needed. Then he'd just do it.

He had no choice. He couldn't let their sickness spread.

Chapter 14

Maddy couldn't sleep, but it wasn't worry or heartache that kept her awake. Anticipation curled in her belly, clawed at her nerves. She waited, and she hungered.

Chase had walked her back to her house right after dinner. On her porch, before going through the door, she'd turned to him, a slight smirk in her voice, and asked, "Work on my computer?"

Chase flashed that grin of his, the one that never failed to flutter her belly and make her smile in return. "I didn't want to tell anyone the truth—that I was coming over to prepare you for me, for later tonight."

She'd taken a quick shower while he watched with a level of intensity that all by itself lit her fires. When she'd dried herself, he ordered her to bend at the waist and lean on the vanity. She rested her upper body on a folded towel he'd placed for her there.

The lubricant felt cool against her hot flesh. While he spread it, he said, "I'd like to take a paddle to that lovely naked ass of yours some time. How do you feel about that?"

Oh, the images! Full color and completely erotic they'd instantly come alive in her mind and had damn near made her come on the spot. She'd never known she would like so many different things, that she could be aroused this way. Unable to speak at first, she could only moan. Chase had dipped a finger into her. Her eyes were drawn to the mirror over the sink. She watched as, behind her, he sucked that finger into his mouth.

"You're nice and wet and very tasty so I'll take that as a yes. I'm telling you right now, it'll sting. But I've found that a bit of pain during sex is one of the best aphrodisiacs in the world. We'll make a special occasion of the first time, maybe have you tied to the bed and completely at our mercy. We'll plan for it."

"Chase."

His chuckle dripped sex. *The things this man does to me with just his voice and his words ought to be illegal.*

"But not tonight. Tonight is for just you and me. Tonight, you're going to take me the way Lucas takes me. The way I take him." And with that, he slid the butt plug into her.

He'd brought her to her bed, told her to lie down on her belly. His hand on her sex had stroked and teased, and Maddy's arousal coated her in a fine sweat. Her hips undulated, and the presence of the plug within her added to the delicious sensations coursing through her. This larger plug she'd only worn one other time. The sensation of it and Chase's fingers both massaging different erogenous zones brought her to the brink.

He didn't let her come, of course. He wanted her burning for him.

"I want you to stay just like this. Naked, needy, and waiting for me. I'll be back in a couple of hours. I have to go have my cake, and then spend some time with Lucas. I'll tuck him into bed and then come to you. Sleep if you can, darling. Because you won't get much of that precious commodity once I return."

She'd been exhausted when she'd left dinner, but all tiredness had fled in the wake of Chase's erotic promise.

She stayed where he'd left her. She didn't have to 'obey' him, she knew that. But when he told her to do something, when he—well, when he played the dominant, something about it and him simply thrilled her. She *wanted* to obey him. She wanted to submit to his will completely. But he only wore the mantle of master in the bedroom.

Outside of it, he had nothing but respect for her authority as the owner of the ranch where he lived and worked. Even inside the bedroom she knew he would never do anything to demean her. This morning, when he'd told her to come back here with Luc, to let that man 'take care of her' while he began to deal with the problem that had been eating at her soul she'd felt an emotion she'd believed could never be hers: complete relief.

She could and would continue to make her own decisions, steer her own course, and face her own consequences in life. But how wonderful to relinquish control for a bit, and feel absolutely safe in doing so!

If that wasn't love, Maddy didn't know what was. She wanted to tell him and Lucas how she felt. She didn't know if they'd be pleased or horrified by her words. The prospect of actually saying them out loud made her more than a bit nervous.

It would be taking one hell of a chance. Of course it would. And yet the glimpse she'd gotten so far of what it could be like to be part of a family—a real family because in many ways that's what the three of them were—had whetted her appetite, teased her into wanting what she'd never allowed herself to want.

Telling those two studs she loved them would be risky. But she—and they—were worth it.

So the next time she had them both here, the next time they stole private time for themselves, she'd tell them.

"There you are."

She hadn't heard Chase come into the house, but the sound of his voice flowed over her naked flesh, the deep sexy timbre the most exquisite sensation she'd ever known.

A moan escaped her soul as he stroked one hand down her back, splayed it over her ass then followed the crack, down along her curves until he brushed the lips of her labia.

"I've brought some candles. I'm going to set them around the room. I want to see you in candlelight."

"Chase. I need you." She didn't mind begging. There could be no ego here, no posturing.

"Of course you do, darling. Because you belong to me. Don't you?"

"Yes. Oh, yes, I belong to you."

"Then you'll have me. You'll have all of me. But there's no rush. We have all night. And darling? I need you too."

Her arousal burned so hot Maddy felt tempted to play with herself, bring about her own orgasm. Instead, she angled her body slightly, bringing her right leg up, bending it at the knee, then holding herself tightly. Flexing the muscles of her perineum felt so good, especially with the butt plug in.

Chase laughed softly. "Horny, darling?"

"I've never been so horny. Every time I think it can't possibly be as good as the time before, but it keeps getting better." That was part of this wondrous miracle. That each day, each moment of each day, improved upon the last.

"And it always will."

That, Maddy thought as she watched him set some of the candles about, light them, had sounded suspiciously like a promise. Then Chase walked over to the door, flicked the overhead light switch, and Maddy's mind turned off.

The room shimmered in a soft, golden glow.

"There, that's better."

Chase came over to the left side of the bed, the side she faced, and slowly began to strip the clothes from his body.

"I expect Lucas will soon be fast asleep. I've already ordered that bed for us, Maddy. It arrives on Saturday. Are you looking forward to having us both in your bed for the entire night?"

The very thought of having them both with her through the night made her insides purr. "Yes. I want you both to stay the night with me. Every night." She wanted them with her, in her, every moment she could have them.

"We'll talk about every night later. For now, do you want to know what I did with Lucas a few minutes ago?"

He had only his jeans left, and Maddy's mouth watered as he peeled the fabric down his legs. *My God, he's so beautiful.* His muscled body glowed even more golden in the candlelight than normal. His cock, long and thick, and a little larger than Luc's stood erect and proud. The wicked gleam in his eye told her he knew she lusted for him, and more, that he approved.

"Yes. Tell me about you and Lucas. I love watching the two of you together. I love knowing that I fit in there with you, and that I'm the only one you share with."

"Oh, darling, very soon you're going to be the meat in our man sandwich. Would you like that? Would you like to have us both fucking you at the same time?"

He came down on the bed beside her and scooped her into his arms. Nearly delirious with the pleasure of his hot, naked flesh against her own she wrapped her arms around his neck, her lips fastening on his. His flavor intoxicated her, the glide of his tongue against her own tasted so good, felt so right, that nothing mattered but this. The subtle sucking sound of his mouth thrilled her. He devoured her and she gloried in it.

"I had Luc's cock in my mouth, as he had mine. He said it excited him to know that so soon after I'd be buried deep inside you. We sucked each other off, talking about how much we enjoy the feel of your naked breasts in our hands and our mouths. We talked about what a thrill it will be to have you watch us fuck each other. Do you know what I want to do? I want to put my mouth on the two of you the next time Luc has his cock buried in your pussy."

His words were the most erotic pillow talk she'd ever heard. Never had Maddy understood the power of words as she did now. When Chase took her mouth again, she thought she might come right then and there. She wanted to be absorbed by him, blur the lines between them so they became one. Her nipples loved the abrasion of the hair on his chest, and she rubbed herself back and forth against him.

"I want all of that. I want everything and anything. I want *you*."

She'd had lovers, but only now dared to be so bold. She'd wanted, but had never demanded and surrendered at the same time. She hadn't known that she could, that it could even be possible. She brought one of his hands to her drenched labia at the same time she arched up and rubbed a nipple against his mouth.

He took her nipple, sucked and nipped as he rolled her on the bed, his fingers moving in and out of her slit in a rhythm both heavy and full. Her hips rose off the bed, begging for more.

His mouth released one nipple only to take the other. His hot moist breath bathed her, aroused her, set her ablaze.

"More. Moremoremoremoremore," the chant became her mantra, a writhing, pulsing need that spread, consuming every whim, every thought.

"You're so hot, so wet," his words vibrated against wet flesh, tingling her skin, chasing shivers down her spine. "I want to drink from you."

Maddy cried out when Chase's mouth found her woman-flesh. His tongue flicked her clit on its way to her tunnel, and with long, slow laps he drank. His lips closed over hers, the suction so marvelous she wondered she didn't melt into the bed. Control evaporated as she came, the sexual chaos overtaking her so thoroughly she collapsed against the pillow, her keening wail coming with each breath, her muscles so lax she couldn't move, her body so surrendered she lay completely splayed and vulnerable.

The sound of foil tearing nearly didn't register. Surging up her body on his way to claiming her, he said, "Here, now, feel what it'll be like with two of us inside you."

She shouldn't have been able to come again, but she did, the hot hard invasion of his cock into her stretching her, the rubber surrogate embedded in her anus feeling fuller and larger with his penetration and pounding.

Chase pumped into her and she gave him all she could, tilting her pelvis to better cradle him. He took her mouth, daring her to sample her own essence on his lips. Maddy devoured it, each new flavor and sensation rocking her to her soul.

Her body shivered in the aftermath of orgasm. Chase slowed his pace, and she understood he hadn't yet come.

"Roll over now, baby. Let me take you now."

He had to help her to turn over, she had little strength left. He must have known, for he placed two pillows under her to help hold her up.

"Tell me, Maddy. Tell me you want this."

"Yes." She wanted him every way she could have him. But she would do more than acquiesce. She would demand.

"Fuck my ass, Chase. Fuck me."

"Maddy."

He pulled the plug out, and the sliding sensation peaked her nipples again. And then she felt him, the latex covered girth of him pressing against her tiny rosebud.

The skin of her anal opening stretched and burned and still she wanted more. She moved her ass, pushed back, wiggled subtly from side to side, and was rewarded with the sound of his hiss, the fierce grip of his hands on her hips, and the slow, steady impalement of her ass with his penis.

"Oh, God, Maddy. So good. *So* good. Does it hurt, baby?"

"Yeah." She couldn't deny the burning, the stretching. "Hurts damn good." Chase had said a slight bit of pain made the best aphrodisiac in the world, and now she knew he'd spoken the truth.

"I'm going to move. I'll try to take it slowly."

Out and in, back and forth, Maddy moaned as her arousal began a slow steady climb for the third time. She was his, completely and totally his, and could deny him nothing. Nothing in life could be better than this, except having Lucas with them, Lucas in her so that the three of them could truly become one flesh.

"Oh, Maddy. Damn, woman you're so hot and tight around my cock."

She felt his trembling, his control. He was being careful of her, gentle, and she loved that. She loved him. Loving him, she wanted to surrender completely. She wanted to give him everything, allow him every freedom, nothing held back.

"Take me. Hard, fast. I want your pleasure. Give it to me. Give me everything."

"*Yes.*"

His hips began to slam against her. He reached one hand down and around, easily finding her clit. He stroked with his fingers while he plundered with his cock, and Maddy rejoiced in the total shedding of civilization, in the glide and slide and clutch and squeeze of her inner beast. He covered her, his arms no longer supporting him, so he lay against her. She bore his weight, bore his possession, and felt his hot heaving breath against her neck. Images of the stallion and mare flashed through her mind, and the sound that came from her traveled from the depths of her soul, from the part of her that held the feral creature of nature.

Chase set his teeth on the curve of her shoulder, his bite just as primitive, his cry of triumph a guttural sound, a fanfare announcing his conquest and his ejaculation.

Maddy reveled in his pleasure, in her own orgasm joining his, as she gave herself over to the miracle of being a woman, and belonging to him.

Chapter 15

"Your woman will think you spent a fortune on her. Unless she takes this baby to get it appraised, she'll never know it's a knock-off. Why, I predict she'll lavish extreme sexual favors all over your person once you give her this."

This was a ring, cubic zirconium set in cheap gold that Kevin was about to spend one hundred and twenty of the five thousand dollars his dear Aunt Verna had given him for this purpose. He frankly didn't give a flying fuck if Maddy thought it a genuine stone or not, as long as it fooled Aunt Verna. And since the old broad's eyes weren't that good these days, he considered the balance of four thousand eight hundred and eighty dollars his for the keeping.

He didn't need a ring to get extreme sexual favors from Maddy, anyway. He only needed a good piece of leather and a strong arm.

It had occurred to him as he'd endured the ritual of dinner last night with his Aunt that he really hated the bitch. He'd been fuming over her latest lecture on frugality—the price for receiving an extra stipend from his own damn money so he could 'do right by that fine young woman', when he'd had a brainstorm. Since he considered Maddy so much like Verna, why not take his anger with his aunt out on her?

That idea had damn near made him come in his pants. Kevin smiled now, and he didn't care if the hawker misread his smile, or not.

"I need a fancy box, too," Kevin told the man as he counted out the cash for the ring.

"For twenty extra, I can give you a ring box from *Destiny*." The seller seemed to have all the bases covered.

"Well worth it." Kevin wrapped up the transaction quickly, and then headed back to his truck. He'd driven all the way to Colorado Springs because no way in hell he'd go to Parkinson's Jewelry store in Marshville. Then he'd *have* to spend the five Gs Verna had handed him, because she'd know if he didn't. A sudden thought made him frown. His aunt might give him grief about going to the big city to buy the ring instead of shopping locally. Then he laughed. He'd tell her that a college friend, just out of the service and back from overseas, had hired on to Destiny and he'd wanted to give the guy's business a boost.

Aunt Verna could be so clueless, it was pathetic. She'd likely fall for that pap and he might even score a few points in the bargain. Kevin pulled out of the parking lot and headed toward the interstate. Today was Friday. In just a couple more days, his future would be assured. All he had to do was avoid speaking with Barnes until then.

He'd kept his cell phone turned off when the sound of its ringing, and the call-display showing a New York area code had gotten on his nerves. For long stretches at a time, he could put Rick Barnes completely out of his thoughts. But then his obligation would come right back and bite him in the ass.

If he doubted for even a minute that he'd be successful in getting Maddy to buckle under and sign over her land, he'd be scared shitless. He'd gone over his plan with a fine tooth comb. No way would it fail.

Maddy was a woman alone, with not so much as a distant relative she could count on for help. Not only that, but the woman hadn't exactly gone out of her way over the last few years to make friends. He doubted even two people in the entire county would take her part in any confrontation against him. Plus, old man Dalton had really been a miserable, mean son-of-a-bitch most of his life. He'd attended the old bastard's funeral, of course. Listening to gossip as he always did—how else did a man keep abreast of things?—he knew most of the people who'd come to that send-off had done so out of curiosity. Damn near everyone said what a blessing the bastard had finally died.

Maddy's age put her over-the-hill with absolutely no prospects, except him. The clincher—he knew the idea of being arrested, going to jail, would terrify the living hell out of her. Shit, that prospect sure terrified him. And she was just a woman, so her terror would that much bigger. He could take that picture to the sheriff—no, to the state police—and it would be his word against hers. He was a pillar of the community and she was—well, she was just a woman.

Kevin patted his inside jacket pocket, the ring's presence there a solid indication that he had everything under control. There would be no limit to what he would be able to do, and have, once he handed the land over to Barnes and collected his fat check.

He gloried in the way his brand new Ford F350 Super Duty Pick-Up ate up the distance between Colorado Springs and home. The miles whizzed past, and Kevin re-affirmed to himself that buying the truck had been as sound a business decision as buying the new Caddy had been.

Both vehicles spoke "success" to different groups of people. His Aunt Verna could never understand this one basic principle: it wasn't enough that you *be* successful, you had to *look* successful. She'd never appreciated that his desire for the best really wasn't vanity, as she always liked to say. It was the implementation of sound business principles.

Before long, he took the exit that would bring him into Marshville. He'd go to his real-estate office before checking in with the seed-and-feed. He'd left instructions with his manager there that he should go ahead and process any order Maddy came into town with. Inquiring about her—whether or not she'd been in, and if so, what she'd purchased—would just cement gossip of his 'courtship' of her. Of course, he'd dropped a few comments here and there already, so that when it became public knowledge that he and Maddy were going to be married, there'd be a general competition among the gossip mongers as to which one of them had 'known all along' first.

He knew how these small-minded, small-town people thought. And knowledge, as his daddy always used to say, equaled power.

He parked in front of his office, giving a smile and a nod—friendly without inviting anyone to actually approach him—and tossing the keys up then catching them, he headed toward his office. He was in one hell of a good mood. Maybe he'd go to that steak house over in Gunnison tonight, have himself a celebratory dinner. Hire himself one of those hookers and pretend she was Maddy, get a little practice in.

Smile on his face, he opened the door to his office, stepped in, and froze. There, sitting where his secretary should have been, loomed one big, bald, tough-looking son-of-a-bitch, a man Kevin had never laid eyes on before. Directing his attention to the right, he could see his inner office door standing open.

Rick Barnes sat in *his* chair, behind *his* desk, and sent Kevin a really nasty smile.

"Ah, Marsh, there you are. Come in. Make yourself at home. Let's talk, shall we?"

* * * *

Lucas had never been comfortable sending his crew out to do what he wasn't willing to take on himself. In this, he and Maddy were of the same mind.

He set his heels to Majesty's sides, content when the gelding raced across the open ground. Pat and Charlie had ridden out to check the pastures to the west, to take a head count of the cattle and look for any signs of feline predators. Chase had stayed back to help Bill and Ralph with the servicing of Selestial. Maddy liked to be on hand for those events, because her horses formed the heart of her business.

It contented Lucas to spend an afternoon on his own, on horseback. He headed toward the east pasture to look for any sign of cougars. He really hoped there weren't any, but if Jordan had spotted one, there would likely be more. Since he was their neighbor to the east, he figured if the cats had made it as far as Circle D land, that's where they'd be.

The old Talbot spread lay between Comstock land and them. Old man Talbot had gone and left the ranch—and a going concern it had once been, too—to his worthless nephew, Kevin Marsh.

As far as Lucas knew, Marsh hadn't set foot on the place since he'd inherited it a few years before. *None of my never-mind.* Still, he hated to see anything go to waste.

The afternoon had turned warm, edging toward hot. The only sounds invading the peace were the sounds of insects and birds, and the occasional far-off bawl of a cow—nature songs that enhanced the tranquility. Nature songs that he'd never taken for granted. He'd always felt lucky to live where he lived, and to be a cowboy.

Lucas knew he could never live in a big city. He didn't, in truth, know how Chase had been able to stand it all those years. But apparently he had, and Lucas worried the younger man would miss the excitement of places like New York and Philadelphia. But Chase had assured him last night that he really wanted to be, and stay, with him and Maddy.

Lucas had never been happier in his life. He never dreamed that he would have one lover, never mind two. And not just lovers but…mates. No other word described what both Chase and Maddy had become to him. They were his mates, and he very much wanted to spend the rest of his life with them.

He didn't know, however, if either one of them felt the same way.

The most amazing aspect of this ménage relationship the three of them had was that Chase and Maddy could be alone together, as they had been for the entire night last night, and Lucas didn't feel the least bit jealous.

True, he'd gotten pretty aroused imagining what the two of them had been doing in Maddy's bed—just as Chase had become aroused when he and Maddy had spent private time together yesterday afternoon. Lucas had dreamt last night, one of the hottest dreams he'd ever had, and figured it due in no small part to thinking of his lovers together. He loved them both, and could only feel joy that they were as drawn and attracted to each other as they were to him.

Lucas adjusted his seat in the saddle, silently cursing himself for letting his thoughts dwell for too long on them. He'd be with them soon enough, and while it didn't hurt to allow the anticipation to build, it wasn't a good idea to be sporting an erection while riding his horse.

Majesty made a huffing noise as if in agreement. He and the gelding had been partners for a long time, however, and Lucas recognized that sound. The horse smelled something unfamiliar.

He reined the animal in, took a moment to look around. He should be coming on the cattle they had in this pasture soon. His eyes sharp, he scanned the area, and even let his gaze wander to the ground. The gelding wasn't skittish, so he knew whatever the horse could sense didn't frighten him.

A small rise of land appeared just ahead of him. On the other side of it, the stream that meandered through this area cut up, and then turned east and crossed over to the old Talbot place. Looking around, he figured it to be about a quarter mile to the edge of Maddy's property.

They'd been careful, ever since Marsh had inherited that land, to make sure they stayed on this side of the boundary. The fence they had strung there had become top priority and got examined closely each spring for defects.

The last thing any of them wanted to do was to give Kevin Marsh just cause to bitch.

Following a gut feeling, Lucas decided he'd ride to the edge of the property. Something had gotten Majesty's attention, and he needed to find out what.

Lucas saw them as soon as he crested the rise.

A Jeep stood parked about a hundred feet from the stream. How it had gotten there became apparent almost immediately, because as Lucas approached he noticed the fence had been cut, the wire peeled back.

He stopped his horse and watched. The men didn't appear to be armed. They seemed only to be interested in the stream.

Quietly, he reached behind him and pulled out the rifle he always carried in the scabbard tied to the back of his saddle. Laying the weapon across his lap, he took up the reins again and nudged his horse forward.

"Good afternoon," he said as he approached the trespassers.

The men looked up, appearing unconcerned at being caught. One of them nodded, but returned his attention to his work. As Lucas drew closer he realized that the man was getting several samples of water from the stream.

"Hi," the second man greeted. "Nice day."

"It is indeed. Do you gentlemen mind telling me what it is you're doing there?"

"Not at all. We've been commissioned to take some water samples, test the purity of the stream. I understand there's a hot spring around here, too, but our directions aren't very clear. We need to get samples of that while we're at it. Maybe you could help us, point us in the right direction?"

"Well now, I'd be glad to do that, but I'm afraid you're trespassing on private property."

"No, it's all right. I assure you, we have the permission of the owner."

"Jerry, go get the work order. It's in my case on the back seat," the older man said from his position at the edge of the grassy bank.

Lucas watched while Jerry walked over to the Jeep. He hadn't completely relaxed, and nudged Majesty slightly so that he could keep both men in sight.

Within moments, however, Jerry came away from the vehicle with some papers in hand, and approached Lucas.

"It's all right here. This work order is signed by Mr. Kevin Marsh, and the water assessment ordered on behalf of the prospective buyer of the property, F.J. Barnes Investments Limited."

Lucas nodded. "Kevin does own some land here. That fence was the border between his land and the Dalton ranch."

"Something's not right." The man who had been testing the water came over to them then, handed Jerry the bottles, and took the paperwork. He flipped through the pages until he came to one, then handed the entire packet up to Lucas.

"See here? That's the old property line, between Mr. Marsh's land, and what used to be the Dalton Ranch. My understanding is that Ms. Dalton has signed over her property to Mr. Marsh, which I suppose is only fitting since they are engaged to be married."

Lucas looked at the map for a long moment. Shaking his head, he handed it back. "Something's not right, all right. And that would be your information, and this map. I'm Ms. Dalton's ranch foreman, and I happen to know none of what you just said is the truth."

"Well, hell." The older man looked over at where he'd cut through the fencing. "I had a feeling when we couldn't find a gate."

"Shit, Patrick. What are we going to do?"

"I don't know," Patrick replied. "We need to call Mr. Barnes." Then he looked up at Lucas. "I guess we owe you for a fence."

Lucas looked over at the broken barrier. He had wire cutters and some spare wire in his saddlebag—he always carried some in case he had to make an emergency repair. He figured this qualified.

"Don't worry about the fence. I'd say that's on Marsh."

The men made quick work of packing up their supplies and heading back across the boundary. It didn't take Lucas more than a few minutes to jerry-rig a patch to the fence. It wasn't the best job, but it should hold until he could send someone back with another piece of wire. Then he mounted his horse, and headed them both in the direction of home.

One thing he knew for certain. Maddy sure as hell was going to be pissed.

Chapter 16

"That slimy little son-of-a-bitch!" Maddy wanted to punch someone. Actually, she wanted to punch Kevin Marsh right in his fat little nose. Since that wasn't an option at the moment, she paced back and forth in her office. She'd never been so angry in her entire life.

Chase sat at the keyboard of her computer, where he'd headed as soon as Lucas had finished recounting his little adventure in the east pasture. Lucas had just returned to the house after sending Pat and Charlie out to fix the newly-compromised fence, and had installed himself in the wing-back chair that faced her desk. Both men seemed determined to stay out of her way while she had her little rant. She appreciated that.

"I knew the bastard wanted my land, but I had no idea he wanted to sell it to a developer!" She stopped and turned to look at both men. "Even with that business with the photo, I thought 'yeah, he's an asshole, but not a terribly clever one'. I mean, the guy's a screw-up, he always has been. But this is different. *This* is going too far."

Lucas shook his head then fixed her with a hard stare. "The threat to throw you in jail wasn't going too far?"

Maddy had blown enough steam that she was finally able to take in the mood of her men. Both of them looked as pissed as she felt. She was out of practice—if she had ever been *in* practice—of taking a lover's feelings into account. Now she realized that she did indeed need to do just that. Both Chase and Lucas had been remarkably restrained, all things considered. But lack of reaction in no way reflected a lack of intense emotions. They were men, and even if they respected her right to fight her own battles, there were limits to the insults to her they'd tolerate.

Maddy responded with honesty and candor. "That scared me. This pisses me off."

Lucas met her gaze for a long moment. "Yeah, all right, I get that. And for the record, us too—on both counts." He turned to look at Chase. "You find anything yet?"

Maddy turned her attention to Chase as well. "Anything what? What are you doing?" It had just occurred to Maddy that she'd accepted Chase's commandeering her computer but had no idea why he'd done so.

Chase looked up from the monitor, his eyes glittering with purpose. By the expression on his face, *he* was way beyond pissed. "An investment company that would undertake this kind of a venture without any kind of due diligence—which is exactly what's happened—can't be on the up and up."

"Oh. Shit."

"Shit, indeed. I'm not real happy with what I'm seeing here, so far. There's not much of a prospectus, not much information on the company, and it's a privately held entity. I can find no list of properties developed, and almost no chatter of any kind."

"So, what do we do?" Maddy asked. It occurred to her then that she'd come a long way in a short while. Not too long ago, she would have insisted on looking at all the information available, weighing her options, then choosing her course of action—all on her own.

But in the last couple of weeks, while she hadn't completely toppled her walls, she had made a door and opened it, allowing these two men in.

She didn't really understand how trusting them with her body had led her to trust them with everything else, too. Except they accepted her, warts and all and didn't appear to want to change her. Get her to relax some, yes; lean on them a little, most definitely. But she knew in her heart they were truly equals in this relationship, for they would lean on her too, if necessary.

"I'm going to call Phil. He's still connected to the Justice Department, and he can let me know if there are any ongoing investigations involving this Barnes character or his company."

"And if there are?"

"Despite what you might think, that would be a positive for our side. We'll have to get in touch with Sean Paris, too. He'll want to know if someone like that had come to play in his back yard, and actually, Kevin's having made this move changes the situation, considerably. Even more so if Barnes is dirty."

"And if he isn't?" There still existed a part of her that just wanted to do something about this entire situation now, and alone. Chase must have seen that in her eyes, because the look he sent her was one of the most tender she'd ever seen.

"One step at a time, darling. We'll cross that bridge if and when we come to it."

"All right." There really wasn't anything more to be done in the moment. She could wish either things moved faster or that she had more patience. But beyond that, she knew everything that could be done, was being done. Of course, that didn't mean she stopped thinking about it.

Maddy continued to pace while Chase spoke to his friend. She couldn't imagine how Kevin could have thought he'd get away with selling her land out from under her. Had he really believed that attempt at blackmail would work? Couldn't he figure out that if worse came to worst, she would pick jail over marriage to him?

Not that long ago she would have said she'd pick jail over marriage to anyone. She didn't feel quite the same way now.

Oh, she knew she couldn't marry either Chase or Lucas, because it would have to be both of them, or neither. Somehow she didn't think the laws of Colorado would change anytime soon to allow for the formalization of ménage relationships. Didn't seem fair to her. Hell, it had never seemed fair to her that couples of the same sex couldn't get married if they wanted to. People had the right to chart their own course, didn't they? The Constitution guaranteed the right to the pursuit of happiness. Why did other people have to dictate the definition of that happiness?

She'd always held marriage was a convenience contrived by some to take advantage of others.

A promise and a vow and a piece of paper.

That's how she'd always thought of marriage. Only now those words took on an entirely new meaning.

"You're tense, darling," Lucas said.

Maddy realized then that Chase had finished his call and both he and Lucas were gazing at her intently.

Just that quickly, she was wet. "So I am. What are you going to do about it?"

The two men exchanged looks and then gave her twin Cheshire-cat grins. Chase got to his feet and came around the desk.

"Why, we're going to do what any concerned and thoughtful lovers would do. We're going to rid you of your tension, of course."

* * * *

Chase had never been an Eagle Scout. Still, he thought he'd done all right.

"Does that hurt?" he asked.

"N...no." Maddy's voice came out just a bit wobbly.

"You're not frightened, darling, are you?" He wanted Maddy off balance, not afraid. She hadn't objected to the ropes they'd used on the hammock, out under that tree. But he suspected ropes in the bedroom seemed an entirely different thing.

"I'm not exactly sure what I am."

Lucas chuckled low and deep, the sound a masculine caress that licked down Chase's spine and settled at the base of his cock. "What you are, Maddy darling, is bound and blindfolded and gloriously naked," his lover said.

"We're going to play with you now, baby." Chase whispered.

Chase lay on the bed on her right and took a long moment to just enjoy the view. Her breasts, plump and firm, had been kissed by a shiver, causing her nipples to peak. Dipping his head down, he captured a bud in his mouth and was immediately rewarded by Maddy's groan.

Lucas, on her left, began to pet her, delivering long slow strokes from her arm—secured over her head and fastened to the brass headboard—all the way down to just above her mound.

Chase smiled as Maddy trembled and twitched.

"Oh, please…give me more." Her plea emerged as a whisper balanced on the edge of desperation.

"We've only just started," Lucas said. The moment Chase released one nipple from his mouth, Luc began to suckle the other one.

"You're so responsive to us, sweetheart," Chase praised, and captured her mouth with is. She tasted of honey and cream, a flavor he knew he'd crave for the rest of his life. A woman of strength, but incredibly feminine, she was everything he'd ever envisioned her to be, and more. She'd turned out to be the perfect woman for him. His tongue delved and swirled, drank her in and plundered.

Chase weaned his lips from hers at the same moment Luc raised his head from her breast. Desire swamped Chase and he leaned forward and kissed him.

A different flavor here, stronger, just as potent, just as vital. Their tongues met and played, Luc's shyness having given way to a fine boldness that thrilled Chase. *They complete me.* How lucky he was to have found the only two people in the world who could.

As if of one mind, they ended their kiss and turned their passion on their woman.

* * * *

They drove her quietly insane.

Restrained, her eyes covered, Maddy's reality became a world of sensation only.

They suckled both nipples at the same time, a powerful stirring of arousal stretching a tight electric current from those pebbled peaks to her womb. They'd stopped talking when they'd stopped touching her long enough to remove their clothes. She didn't know who's hand was where, because the caresses had become fleeting, teasing. Could she stand any more? *Oh God, yes.*

Something soft, like fur, brushed against her belly, dipping down to gently stroke against her woman flesh. Maddy cried out, flexing her hips, trying to capture the illusive touch. Low, masculine laughter washed over her then, and she tried to figure out who lay on which side, but couldn't. A gentle stroke against the side of her face made her turn in that direction. Her lips were captured in a kiss hot, wet and carnal. *Lucas.* Two men, two different flavors, both lip-smackingly delicious. Then he withdrew, replaced by Chase, whose tongue demanded and commanded, then he was gone just as fast.

Desire dominated, controlled, begged. "More."

How could it thrill her so to beg, and to be denied? How could she feel free while being restrained and controlled? She couldn't force this, couldn't command an orgasm as she did when she masturbated, something to be slid into her busy schedule before rushing off to the next task. She could only lie here and take whatever they wanted to give her, all they wanted to give her, and luxuriate in the sense of soaring liberation that filled her.

The caresses resumed, sweeping bold touches that ended in a tight grasp of flesh, or feather-light kisses like butterfly-wings, barely there, yet brazenly erotic. They teased her, nearly petting her damp folds. *Nearly.* Close, not close enough, so she stretched, pushed her hips up, seeking, pleading. There, just *there*, and, ah yes, delving deep, strong fingers, surrogates for strong cocks. Then gone again, leaving her near madness, panting and desperate.

Back and forth across her slit, a gentle rubbing brought her clit to attention. She strove toward it, a pinching of her nipple now in concert with that rub, the pressure increasing, until it almost became painful. Warm breath stirred the mouth-dampened skin of her breasts, a similar breeze caressed her woman flesh, and Maddy's panting increased as rapture danced coquettishly close, then skittered away.

She was taken hold of by strong hands, turned onto her right side. The heat of a male body pressed against her back, her left leg pulled up and over a hirsute male thigh. One hand came from behind and cupped her breast, squeezing possessively. A hot, hard cock slid into her pussy from behind, surging deep.

"Yes...oh yes, please, *harder*." Desperate to come, her hips tried to piston, but instead were restrained by firm masculine hands. The image flashed in her mind, her imagination keen to replace denied vision, of one lover behind her, buried deep within her, fucking her, while another lay before her, holding her steady while he watched. Her heart pounded fast in her chest, every nerve ending in her body sizzled and snapped, and arousal surged, a hot spiral of need that climbed and climbed to impossible heights.

Slow, sultry thrusts inside her, stretching her, burning and chilling, her hands unable to move, her eyes unable to see, so that there was only this, only the firm grasp of her breast in a callused hand, and the hot, hard, deep thrusting of a lover's cock into her pussy, the flexing of strong fingers on her hips, and hot, hot breath against her mound.

Masculine lips descended on her then, moved back and forth over her labia, as a tongue lapped and tasted and drank of them both, woman and man. Teeth captured her clit, delivering it to the hot moist cavern of a mouth. Long, and deep, he sucked on her nub.

Maddy screamed as she came, screamed and bowed and writhed as she was held strong, held fast. No escape, no ease, just a wild, harsh, electrifying ride that went on and on until she thought she might faint, on and on as the climax crashed, ebbed, then built again.

* * * *

"Sweetheart?"

Maddy surfaced briefly, the sensation of blankets being pulled up and tucked around her, the warmth and the comfort of them urging her to return to sleep.

"I'd say we took care of her stress problem."

Masculine smugness. She opened her eyes, blinked. She must have slept, for she was no longer tied to the bed or blindfolded. But she *was* alone in her bed.

"Where are you going?" Was that her, sounding needy, almost whiny? It didn't matter, did it, if they knew she needed them, because she knew they needed her, too.

There wasn't much light, which told her she'd slept for a while already, and it had turned to night.

"We're going to let you get some sleep," Lucas said softly. He bent down and kissed her lightly. "You're exhausted."

"And tomorrow the new bed arrives. So tomorrow night, you'll have us both to snuggle with. But Luc's right, you are exhausted."

She almost denied that, but her yawn swallowed the words.

"Okay."

"We're going back to my place," Lucas said, "have a few beers and watch a movie. Can we get you anything before we leave?" Luc's question sounded far away, and Maddy felt herself drifting back to sleep. She did want something, but could only say "Window."

"She likes the window open," Luc explained.

Maddy thought Chase might have said something, but a soft evening breeze danced across her face just then, and she fell fast asleep.

Maddy didn't know what had awakened her. She blinked, feeling disoriented. Slowly she realized she lay in her own bed, and alone. The afternoon's activities flooded her memory, and she smiled. Their intention had been to rid her of her tension, and man, had they ever succeeded there. Turning her head, her gaze sought her bedside clock. The green LCD glowed in the darkness proclaiming three-thirty a.m.

An orange glow reflected against the wall at the same instant she smelled the smoke.

Catapulting from her bed, she spun toward the window even as her hands reached for her jeans. Terror froze her arm in mid reach.

Lucas's house was on fire.

Chapter 17

Chase coughed, struggling to rise from sleep, his mind foggy, jumbled. Something prickled his nose and he tried to brush it away but his arms felt too heavy and he was so very tired.

Whisper thin images floated across his mind, calling to him. Maddy, spread out on her bed, naked, needy. Lucas, his cock rigid and ready, his strong arms outstretched as he reached for him. The images pulled at him, seducing him to come back to them, to the realm of sleep and dreams where they awaited him. *Where they'd be his forever.* Yes, he wanted them to belong to him forever. He nearly gave in then, nearly listened to the siren call whispering in his mind.

But something was wrong, dreadfully, horribly wrong.

Chase coughed again, and the taste of smoke, rancid ugly smoke seared his nostrils, coated the inside of his mouth. Struggling, he opened his eyes. They immediately began to water and sting. He shook his head, harsh reality exploding as he realized what was happening.

Fire!

Rolling to his side, he fell to the floor. The air was slightly clearer there, allowing him to inhale, focus, and get his bearings. He'd fallen off the sofa, where he must have fallen asleep while watching television. Yes, he remembered. He'd stayed up late watching DVD movies with Lucas after coming back from Maddy's.

Lucas! Where the fuck was Lucas?

Chase shook his head, trying to think. Not on the sofa. Had he gone back over to Maddy's?

No. Threads of a conversation surfaced in his memory, of Lucas trying to rouse him, then giving up and telling him goodnight. Telling Chase goodnight as he'd gone off to bed.

The smoke thickened and Chase could hear the hiss and crackle of the flames. Terror filled him as he realized the worst of the blaze was toward the other end of the house, the end that had the bedrooms—and Lucas.

Frantic, Chase crawled in that direction, heedless of the danger. The urge to stop, to give in to the coughing was strong, but he willed himself to push on. The smoke was so thick he couldn't see ahead, but on hands and knees he followed the route in his memory, down the hall to the first room on the right.

The bed stood well inside the room, directly across from the door. Chase found it with his head. Scrambling, one hand reached up, searching, searching.

There! Chase's hand connected with a denim-covered leg. He shook it, hard, trying to call out his lovers' name as he did, but choking on the breath he inhaled to do so. The leg moved, a twitch that flooded relief into Chase's soul. Reaching up with his other hand, he grabbed the waistband of Luc's jeans and pulled hard.

"Chase."

His name, weakly whispered and wrapped in coughing sounded sweeter than the most stirring symphony. Chase kept tugging and Lucas must have understood, for he heaved himself toward him.

Lucas came off the bed, landing partly on Chase, mostly on the floor.

"Fire." Though raspy, Lucas's one word told Chase the man was conscious and coherent.

"Yeah, the fucking house is on fire. We have to crawl."

"Maddy?"

"No, sweetheart, Maddy's safe."

A loud crack exploded above them. Chase pulled Lucas, urgency bordering on panic. He couldn't see the doorway, could only sense his way and pray he wasn't completely disoriented in the smoke.

His shoulder hit the door frame just as another loud crack exploded. A gush of air brought flames that licked behind and toward them.

Chase didn't think they were going to make it.

Quitting wasn't an option. Just as he began to sag, Lucas prodded him.

"Keep going. Side window."

Chase understood immediately. The side window in the parlor stood furthest away from the flames, which already lapped and sizzled close to the front door. The house, constructed of wood frame and over fifty years old, likely wouldn't last much longer. Chase maneuvered them in a straight line, down the hall, across the parlor. His eyes burned, his throat burned, and terror coated his skin and lined his bowels. The entire structure around them was ablaze, only the center of the building, where they crawled, remained as yet untouched. But they didn't have much time.

Chase kept moving, kept checking to see that Lucas stayed with him. Ahead, it seemed as if the smoke darkened, solidified. Reaching out, Chase connected with a wall. Luc had stopped, his choking cough so fierce Chase knew he could no longer move forward under his own steam.

Praying harder than he had in his whole life, stepping out on blind faith, Chase struggled to his feet, reached down, lifted Lucas to his, and then heaved them both forward.

* * * *

"Luc! Chase!" Either Maddy's screams, or the screams of the horses had awakened the rest of her crew. The men had come stumbling out of the bunkhouse in various states of undress. Luc's house was closer to the bunkhouse than to her own, so the rest of the men reached it ahead of her.

"Luc! Chase!" *Oh God, oh God. Where were they?* She had to get in there, had to get to them. With her entire focus on reaching her lovers she saw no one else until male arms wrapped around her, stopped her short.

Bill Campbell yanked her back, his grip stronger than she would have thought possible. He must have known her intent, for he yelled, "Maddy, no! You can't go in there."

"Let me go! Let me go!" Struggling, screaming, she fought to get free, to get to her lovers, to save them. A loud sound burst into the air as sparks shot up and out. The window facing the barns had exploded.

Lucas's bedroom window.

"Easy. You can't help them. No one can help them now."

No, she wouldn't believe that. She *couldn't* believe that. "Damn it, let me go!" Maddy clawed at the arms that held her fast. Everything in her struggled as her feral instincts surged up from the depths of her soul.

"Maddy, stop it! Stop! They're just a couple of queers. A couple of *faggots*. They're not worth it! Let them burn!"

"Bastard, let me go!" All she knew, everything inside her, needed to get free, to rescue her lovers. *Her mates.* Desperation clawed within her, and she kicked and scratched and swore. Bill's muffled curse was drowned out when another crack exploded. Maddy watched, horrified, as part of the roof—the part over the master bedroom—collapsed.

"No!" Her voice, nearly hoarse from screaming, choked on her tears. "Fuck you, bastard, *let me go!*"

"Fine, then. Go. Go and die with them, faggot lover!"

The strange words didn't matter, all that mattered was he'd let her go. Running toward the house, the heat of the flames punched out at her before she'd taken five steps.

"Luc! Chase!" *Oh God, if they die, I want to die too!*

"Over there!"

Charlie had come running from the bunkhouse, streaking across the ground, obviously looking for some way to get in. He'd raced across Maddy's path just moments before, and now pointed to the other side of the house.

Maddy looked up just in time to see someone tumble through the side window.

Changing course, she ran, and with Charlie knelt down, reached out.

"Thank God, thank God, thank God." The litany tumbled from her lips. Both men sprawled beneath the window, coughing and hacking and *alive*.

"I'll get Luc, he seems worse off. Help Chase. Move, Maddy, now!" Charlie ordered.

Charlie slipped an arm under Lucas, slung him up in a fireman's carry. Maddy got her arm under Chase's shoulder, pulling and prodding as she struggled to her feet.

"Come on, cowboy. We're not out of danger yet. One foot in front of the other."

"Nag, nag, nag." The croak of his voice was the sweetest sound she'd ever heard.

Maddy felt the tears running down her cheeks, but couldn't give in to the urge to cry. Not yet. He was built solid, and under normal circumstances she knew she could never lift him.

Terror gave her extra strength.

In the distance, the wail of sirens screamed toward them. Maddy finally tumbled to her knees, Chase falling with her, but they'd come far enough away from the fire to be safe.

"Luc."

Chase's voice came out gravelly hoarse, but Maddy knew what he wanted, what he needed. The same thing she wanted and needed, too.

"He's okay. He's coughing his lungs out over there, but he's okay. We have to manage to go just a little farther if we want to be with him. Can you make it?"

"Yeah."

She struggled to her feet, dragging Chase with her. Together they stumbled forward, collapsing again on the ground next to Lucas.

Soot covered her men and they stank like fire. But Maddy had never seen anything so wonderful in all her life as her two lovers, safe. Alive.

Close. That had been way too close. Her gaze was drawn to the blaze. With a swoosh and a roar, flames shot out the window her men had so recently escaped from. She'd nearly lost them. A few seconds slower in moving, and she would have been alone for the rest of her life.

Alone wasn't how she wanted to be any more.

She'd wanted to tell them earlier, but had been afraid—afraid to open herself up completely. Maddy sensed that after this, she would likely never really be afraid again. There would be no more waiting for tomorrow to say it, and no more waiting for one or the other of them to say it first. Damn them to hell, they'd both made her fall in love with them, so if her words made them uncomfortable, that was just too fucking bad. They'd have to learn to live with it. And her.

"Bastards, don't you dare die on me, either of you. I love you both."

* * * *

Lucas figured an abundance of sex, late nights, and beer had saved their lives. If not for all of the above, Chase would have been in bed with him, and they'd likely both be dead.

Lying on the ground, he turned his head to watch the firemen finish dousing the flames that had been near to going out anyway.

They'd gutted the house completely, eating damn near every inch of fuel available.

His eyes still stung even though the firemen had irrigated them. His chest and throat burned like a son-of-a-bitch but he was alive, thanks to Chase. He closed his eyes, the ventilator on his face as well as the pain in his throat discouraging talk.

Next to him, Chase sat on the ground, his own ventilator now pushed aside, one hand on Maddy's shoulder, one on his. *That had been too fucking close.* Luc closed his eyes and simply abided with his loved ones.

It seemed like only moments later he felt something cold on his chest. He opened his eyes to the sight of one of the paramedics bent over him, listening to his chest with a stethoscope. The man looked too damn young to be a professional. *Hell, just about everyone looks young these days.*

"How is he?" Maddy's voice sounded almost as hoarse as Chase's.

"His chest is clearing. His breathing sounds better. To be on the safe side, he should spend at least the rest of the night in hospital."

Lucas shook his head 'no'. No way in hell he would be separated from his family. Not after nearly losing them.

"If we watch him carefully, can he stay here?" Maddy asked.

The paramedic looked over at what was left of Lucas' house. Maddy huffed out a breath, and he nearly smiled. Oh, his woman had no patience for stupid people at all. He really loved that about her.

"In the house behind us. There's a bed there, and everything."

"Maddy."

Chase's voice sounded better than the last time he'd heard it. Lucas smiled. He imagined Chase would spend the rest of their lives being the voice of reason amongst them. At least, Lucas hoped it would be the rest of their lives.

"Yeah, if you're going to keep an eye on him, he can stay here."

Maddy looked so worried, it pulled at Luc's heart. Lifting the mask he said, "Right here." Her soft laughter as she recognized her own words tossed back at her wrapped around him, more soothing than any lozenge.

"Can you sit up, Lucas?"

He nodded then put his own muscles into the effort to supplement the paramedic's strength.

"Dizzy?" the attendant asked.

He was a little, but decided to lie about it. He didn't want to take the chance of anyone changing their mind about sending him to the hospital. "No."

"Just sit still a moment, it will pass."

So much for thinking the paramedic too young. He seemed to be old enough to have Lucas's number.

John Anderson, the fire chief from the company over in Gunnison, came toward them from the wreckage of the house, the expression on his face grim. A man Lucas had played poker with a time or two, John had been a volunteer fire fighter for more than twenty years before he finally accepted the job of chief. He nodded to Maddy and Chase then got down on his haunches, putting him on eye level with everyone.

"We're going to call in a special investigator from over in Colorado Springs to go over the scene. But from what I can tell right now, it looks as if this fire was deliberately set. You piss anybody off lately, Lucas? Win one too many poker pots?"

Lucas's thoughts zeroed in on one target and one target only. Before he could say anything, Chase spoke up.

"If that fucking little pecker-head did this I'm going to personally kick his nuts up so high he'll need to wear a jock strap on his nose."

"What little pecker-head?" Anderson asked.

"That fucking little prick, Kevin Marsh."

Lucas could feel the waves of fury rolling off Chase. He couldn't blame him one bit for it. He figured between them, they'd very likely kill the little bastard.

"Verna Marsh's nephew? From right here in Marshville?"

"Yeah. That little—"

"No."

Maddy's one word stopped Chase cold. Her hand squeezed Lucas' shoulder. He turned his attention to her, but she scanned the area all around them, as if searching. Her next words confirmed it.

"Where's Bill?"

Charlie and Pat stood nearby. Even Ralph was there, all of them witnesses to the night's events.

Lucas couldn't see Bill anywhere.

"Where's Bill?" Maddy asked again, her voice hoarse but frantic. Charlie must have heard, because he stepped forward.

"I thought he went over to the Bunkhouse to make coffee for everyone, but come to think of it, but that was a while ago now."

"Go look. Please."

Charlie must have read something in Maddy's expression, because he swore, then took off at a run toward the bunkhouse.

"What's that all about?" Anderson voiced the question on Lucas's mind.

Maddy was shaking. Chase put his arm around her, held her close. Maddy reached for Lucas's hand, and he gave it to her. Then she turned her attention to the fire chief.

"When I…when I came running out, saw the fire, I wanted…I was going to go in there, I had to get in there to get to them. But he wouldn't let me. Bill wouldn't let me. I fought him. I fought him hard."

"Damn it all to hell, Maddy. What the hell were you going to do, brave the flames to save us?" Chase's chastisement lost some of its punch since his voice sounded so weak and he coughed in the middle of it.

"And you wouldn't do the same thing, positions reversed?" Her expression looked so fierce when she said that, Lucas's heart turned over in his chest. *I love you both* she had said the moment he and

Chase had been dragged clear of the flames. He hadn't said it back. But he would. The moment they were all alone together, he would say it to the both of them.

"That's different. Yeah, yeah, I'm a male chauvinist pig. Sue me. Now tell us what has you so worked up about Bill."

Maddy's eyes glistened with tears and she met Chase's gaze and then his before turning back to Anderson. "He finally let me go. But before he did—oh God, I can't believe this—before he did, he said 'they're just a couple of queers, they're not worth it'. And he…he acted as if he believed them already dead."

Which meant Bill had known they were there together. Lucas acknowledged the shaft of pain as he realized a man he'd known for more than twenty years, a man he'd called friend, had tried to kill him, tried to kill Chase.

Anderson didn't even so much as give either Lucas or Chase an off glance. If hearing that someone he'd known for years was gay bothered the chief at all, he didn't show it. Instead, he turned to look at the smoldering building behind him. As Charlie approached, Anderson got to his feet.

"Bill's not here," the man reported. Bewilderment filled his voice as he continued. "He's not here, and most of his stuff is gone. I checked out back. His truck is gone, too. What the fuck, Maddy? *Bill?*"

Anderson looked from Charlie to Maddy. Then he reached for his cell phone.

"Sheriff Barclay? Chief Anderson. I'm out at the Dalton spread. I have a suspected case of arson to report."

Chapter 18

Maddy invited the men from the bunkhouse up to the ranch house where she proceeded to make them bacon, sausages and eggs. They'd tucked Lucas into bed almost immediately, but Chase refused to rest, claiming he felt good enough to throw together some biscuits, so they had those too, along with lots of coffee.

A somber mood lay over them, and no one felt much like talking. The sun was just cresting the horizon when Chase got up and poured everyone a second cup of coffee. He'd taken the time to shower, but Maddy hadn't. Still wearing a night shirt tucked into her jeans and no shoes, she imagined she looked like hell, but she didn't care.

There was nothing so urgent that it had to be done that day. Maddy gave Charlie and Pat the day off. She called the K-Temple ranch and spoke with Michael Templeton. Rumor and gossip traveled faster than the wind amongst cattle and horse folk, and she wanted them to hear the news of the near-disaster from her, rather than from the grapevine. She offered to send their horse and their man back early, but the Templetons assured her they had no worries about security. When she admitted that she had one mare left to service, Michael told her to go ahead and finish with the planned mating.

Lucas was asleep in her father's bed, face down because he'd neglected to tell anyone that he'd burned the backs of his legs. Against Lucas' protests, she'd called Doc Morton and he'd been kind enough to come out right away.

The burns weren't serious, and not even likely to blister. Doc had applied a topical salve, and also left some pain killers in case Lucas needed them.

Lucas, exhausted, had bitched half-heartedly about having to lie there all alone, but soon tumbled deeply into sleep.

After the early breakfast, Maddy insisted Chase climb into her bed. It stood as a measure of his exhaustion, now that everything that could be done had been done, that he gave her only a token protest. He'd been snoring in minutes. She quickly showered, taking just long enough to clean the smell of smoke and fear from her body. Then it pleased Maddy to spend the rest of the day, until late afternoon, alternating between the rooms, keeping an eye on both her men.

"Hey, pretty lady."

Maddy opened her eyes and yawned. She'd fallen asleep in the wing-back chair that had been a staple in her father's room since he'd first taken sick. There had been times in the past when she'd fallen asleep here, watching over her dad.

But it had been much more poignant keeping vigil over one of the men she loved. The long night must have finally caught up with her. She didn't remember falling asleep.

She blinked and focused on Chase, whose soft words had just awakened her. He hunkered down in front of her, gently stroking her leg. Her eyes swept over to the bed and encountered Lucas's sleepy gaze.

"Hey. Must have fallen asleep. Sorry." She stretched and sat up straighter.

"You're more than entitled. Our new bed should be arriving shortly. Then we can all get cozy together for awhile." Chase's voice sounded much better than it had just hours before.

"For more than a while. You'll stay here from now on. Both of you."

"We need to talk about that, sweetheart." Chase's tone was quiet, with no hint of humor whatsoever. "You mentioned wanting us to live in this house with you once before. But as was made abundantly clear just a few hours ago, some people take great exception to other people living alternate life-styles."

Maddy couldn't help it. Her temper ignited. "Oh, fuck that! Just fuck it. One sick bastard lets hate turn him into a monster, and you want me to change how I want to live my life? I don't think so."

"Maddy. Bill was our friend. We don't know what happened to make him—"

She looked over at Lucas, and her heart simply lurched. He could have been killed, and yet here he lay trying to defend the man who, in all likelihood, had set that fire.

"Lucas, I know you were closer to him than any of us. And I know that what he did has to be devastating to you. But if he could set that fire, then he wasn't really our friend, not ever. He hid a side of himself, a side that I would have found repugnant even *if* the three of us weren't lovers. And I for one refuse to give in to the whims of hate-mongers. I will *not* let small minded people dictate how I live my life."

"Be sure, Maddy." Chase's words nearly shook with passion. His eyes glittered brightly, and she understood in that moment how very much he wanted to accept her offer.

"Be very sure. Because when word gets out that the three of us are living together as lovers—as a family—you may find life outside of the ranch changes, and not for the better."

Maddy's gaze met Chase's for a long moment. She reached for his hand, and he gave it. Then she stretched her other hand out, linked fingers with Lucas. She'd said it only once, and she planned to say it again and again until they really believed it. Until they understood that nothing, *nothing* in her life would ever be more important than the two of them. "I love you both, and I really don't give a rat's ass what anyone has to say about it. I love you, Chase. I love you, Lucas. And that's forever."

"Yeah, about that."

Maddy's heart jumped to her throat when Lucas said those three words. She turned her attention to him, and nearly smiled at the look of discomfort on his face. She knew that look, and it had nothing to do with his recent minor injuries.

"I'm not good with words. Never had to be. I've made my living with my hands and the strength of my back. And until recently, I never had a reason to *want* to be good with words."

Maddy nearly jumped when Lucas pushed himself up. She wanted to stop him, to make him stay lying down. He maneuvered himself until he could sit, with his legs dangling. The position must have been uncomfortable. But she sat there, and let him be his own boss.

"I never thought I'd be able to say this without reservation. I'm in love with you. Both of you. It's not traditional, and hell, more than likely not even socially acceptable *anywhere*. Doesn't matter, I've never been much of a social animal, anyway. But you suit me. You both suit me. And that's that."

"You're both braver than I am." Chase got to his feet, paced halfway to the door and back. "Hell, I came *home* because of the two of you. But I was afraid to say it first. I intentionally manipulated us together, took absolute advantage of your attractions to each other and to me to get my way without even considering actually laying my heart on the line like you two have just done."

Maddy's attention never left Chase. He flushed, and no one said anything for a long moment.

"Pussy."

Maddy laughed so hard she thought she'd fall out of her chair when Lucas said that.

"Well, yeah, kind of, when you think about it," Chase agreed, trying not to laugh.

"You still haven't said it, cowboy," Maddy pointed out.

"I haven't?"

"Come on, lover, swallow it down and spit it out," Lucas said. "No pun intended."

They all laughed for a moment. Then Chase's expression sobered as he looked at her and Lucas for a long moment. The he looked away briefly, and let his gaze wander out the window. When he turned back, his expression had turned more serious than Maddy had ever seen it.

"I love you, Maddy. I love you, Lucas. And that's for keeps. And in about an hour, I'm going to show you both *exactly* how much."

"Why in an hour?" Lucas asked.

"Because the truck carrying our new bed is coming down the driveway. I figure it'll take us at least that long to get it in and set it up."

* * * *

He meant to show them how much he loved them, and they turned the tables on him. He'd patted himself on the back for thinking to order sheets and blankets with the bed. It hadn't taken very long to get things done. Charlie and Pat had lent a hand, and they'd put the old bed in the extra bedroom that Maddy had left empty for years, setting up the new king-sized one in Maddy's room.

Three bedrooms, three beds. Each of them could have their own space, when they needed it. Two could have private time, when they wanted it. But now, because they could, they would spend this night wrapped in each other's arms, all three of them.

He turned to say something to them, and found speech deserted him. They wore equal expressions—more than passion, more than love.

Lucas reached out to him first. With a hand that trembled, he stroked Chase's face with a touch so tender, it nearly brought tears to his eyes.

"You saved my life. You put yourself in danger to save my life."

Chase saw gratitude, of course, but he realized Lucas was expressing more than that. His tone held wonder—maybe a wonder that encompassed all they had become to each other, the three of them. That they had found each other, and real happiness and love when really, the odds had been against that ever happening.

Chase felt that sense of wonder, too.

"How could I not? I can't do without you. I love you."

Lucas's grin flashed, a tad lopsided. "Gets easier the more you say it, huh?"

"Yeah, it does. Especially when you know you're *safe* saying it."

Chase looked from Lucas to Maddy. Their woman was waiting and watching, her smile soft.

"That's the biggest treasure here. We're all safe. We're all...one." Maddy's whispered words settled in his heart.

Lucas stepped closer and kissed him. Gentle and tender, questing and seductive, Lucas's lips courted and his tongue wooed. Smitten, seduced, Chase gave himself over to the sensual delight of exploring Lucas's mouth, one hand resting on the side of his face, returning a caress filled with the love overflowing from his heart.

Fingers opened the buttons of his shirt, and Maddy's hands sought his chest, her touch bold and demanding.

Between them, his lovers undressed him before they undressed themselves.

Soft sipping kisses and gentle caresses awakened and aroused not only his body, but his mind and his spirit. They urged him onto the surface of the bed, and *God*, how wonderful to be between them and be surrounded by their passion and their heat.

"No, let us," Maddy whispered when he would have returned the caresses and the love. She took his hand and laid it beside his head. Then she licked and tasted him, his face and neck and chest. Lucas kissed the other side of his neck while his hand began to stroke his cock, the rhythm slow and sure.

Chase's heart raced and his blood heated as his lovers moved down his body, sipping him with their lips and tongues. The feather-light brush of fingers across his abdomen, dipping into his navel; the callous roughened stroke on the inside of his thigh, down, then up again. Sweet sultry open-mouthed kisses on his collarbone and his pecs. Saucy nips of teeth on his nipples and his neck. Chase couldn't hold back his groans, or the need to touch when Lucas's brown hair brushed the edge of his hip just before he took Chase's cock into his mouth. Maddy's mouth was equally busy, and when she urged him to bend his right knee and move his leg to the side, he complied easily, groaning in bliss when she licked and teased his scrotum. His arousal grew languidly, a gentle rippling cascade of erotica swirling throughout his body, tempting, teasing. Warm, enticing, exciting, and slow.

In perfect sync, Lucas took his cock deep while Maddy sucked his balls into her mouth.

"Oh, *God!*" Chase cried out as he came, the orgasm exploding stronger and penetrating deeper than anything he'd ever experienced before. He bowed off the bed but hands—male and female—held him down, so all he could do was lie there and let it take him. Let them take him.

Wasted, empty, Chase closed his eyes, trying to catch his breath yet not wanting to fully release the amazing climax slowly ebbing away.

"He looks done." *Lucas's voice.*

"Mmm, he does, doesn't he?" *Maddy's.*

"Right here." The least he could do was fire familiar words back. He only wished those words held more strength.

"Are you sure? Maybe we sent you to another plane of existence."

Man, he loved that self-satisfied smirk in Maddy's voice. He loved that her confidence as a woman had grown, and that he'd had a hand—not to mention a couple of other body parts—in helping her make that happen.

"I'm here, and I've just had a fabulous orgasm. But unless I missed something, neither of you did." He opened his eyes and grinned, his gaze meeting first one and then the other of his lovers.

"You didn't miss anything," Lucas said as he stroked a hand up and down Chase's chest. "We just thought we'd wait until you recovered so you could tell us what to do."

He knew his eyes gleamed brightly. "Did you, now?"

"Mm. We both know how much you love to play the dominant. And it does come as some surprise to us both that we love to let you." Maddy's response excited him, just when he believed he was totally replete.

"Oh, man, I have *got* to get me that paddle." Chase looked to see what their reaction to that threat was. Lucas looked interested but Maddy's eyes fairly crossed. Lucas noticed that, of course, and Chase could see his interest turn sharper.

"Maybe I'll buy you one for your birthday," Lucas said.

Chase gazed down at Lucas's cock. Erect and proud, it awaited his command. Chase moved closer to Lucas, giving Maddy more room.

"On your hands and knees, woman." He smiled when she obeyed, treating him to the sight of her breasts hanging, nipples taut, nearly right over his hand.

"Lucas, hand me a condom out of the box."

Chase took the proffered packet, tore it open. Then he reached down, stroked his lover's flesh, and rolled the condom in place.

"On your knees behind Maddy. But don't touch her. Not yet."

When Lucas was in place, Chase knelt on the bed beside them. He reached a hand out, and gently stroked Maddy's opening, back and forth, his fingers light.

"Oh, sweetheart, you're so wet. Are you horny?"

"Yes, I am. Helping you come turned me on. I really want to come too, Chase."

He took Lucas's cock in hand, stroking gently, and when Lucas leaned into that stroke, urged him closer to their woman.

"Do only what I tell you," he whispered.

He placed Lucas' latex-covered penis at the very opening of Maddy's pussy, and kept his hands there as he said, "In, Lucas. All the way in, then out slowly, and then once again. But do not come, either of you."

Seeing, directing, feeling his lovers pleasure each other was a new high for him, something he'd never experienced. They both quivered, and when he told Maddy to hold still, she whimpered with need, but complied.

"Stop, Lucas. Withdraw from her." Lucas groaned, but he, too, complied.

"Oh, yeah, got to have that paddle." He took hold of Lucas, and brought him to Maddy's anus. He rubbed Luc's erection back and forth over the rosebud until both his lovers groaned with need.

"Maddy, baby? Tell Lucas what you want him to do, sweetheart."

"Oh, *please*...Lucas please put your cock inside me. Right there."

Lucas's glittering gaze speared Chase, and Chase felt such heat, and such love, that he knew in that moment, finally, he was complete. Lucas wanted desperately to do just what Maddy had begged him to do, but he waited for Chase to give him permission.

"How do you want him to take you, Maddy?"

"Hard. Fast and hard. Oh, *please!*" Her plea sounded ragged and he knew she balanced on the edge of her climax, hovering just a few breaths away from it.

"Do it, Lucas. Give our woman what she wants."

"Oh, *damn!*" Lucas's guttural cry emerged as he sank his cock deep into Maddy's ass. Hard and fast so that the bed shook, Lucas gave Maddy what she needed, what they both needed. Chase kissed Lucas, a fast hungry little kiss then leaned down to take Maddy's mouth in turn.

And he watched, happy, satisfied, as his lovers both erupted in rapture.

Chapter 19

Sean Paris wasn't at all what Maddy had expected.

Since she'd entered her forties it seemed to her that all the people with whom she dealt on a regular basis—the bank teller, store clerks, and even her dentist—had to be getting younger. Sean Paris, an attorney with the Attorney General's office, looked like a teenager.

Of course, she knew he wasn't.

His ability to keep his cards close to his vest certainly seemed seasoned. Watching him she had no idea whatsoever whether he had come with good news for her, or bad.

When he'd gotten out of his car he'd taken one look at the blackened shell of Lucas's house and immediately demanded to know what had happened. Then, of course, he'd had to get on the phone to Sheriff Barclay, insisting on being apprised as to the status of the investigation. She hadn't characterized what had happened last night as a hate crime, but that's exactly what it had been, and what Paris called it. Hate crimes, Mr. Paris had then informed her, were definitely the aegis of the Attorney General of Colorado.

By the time they'd all made it to Maddy's kitchen table, Maddy felt a wreck, waiting to hear what Mr. Paris had to say with regard to the situation involving that damning photograph and the threat from Kevin Marsh.

"You sit, sweetheart. I'll make coffee."

Lucas's hands on her shoulders, the soft tone and gentle squeeze helped settle her some. That all went out the window the moment Paris opened his attaché case, pulled out a tape recorder, set it on the kitchen table and turned it on.

He spoke by rote, reciting the date, time, and location, as well as noting the names of all present in the room. He must have seen something in Maddy's expression when he looked up, for he immediately turned off the recorder.

"Ms. Dalton, the State of Colorado has no interest in, or any intention of bringing charges against you for anything."

"Oh, thank God." The air totally went out of her and she laid her head on the table for a long, quivering moment.

"Sweetheart, you didn't really think he'd come here to arrest you?" Chase obviously felt bad he hadn't realized the extent of her fears, and she supposed she had no one to blame for that but herself. She hadn't really let her men know exactly how frightened she'd been when they'd got that call this morning informing them of the official's impending visit.

Maddy hadn't really let them in, so they hadn't known to ease her mind. Reversing the habits of a lifetime wouldn't be easy. She would have to do better if she wanted this relationship to work.

Chase rubbed her back, with Lucas standing beside her on her other side, his hand on her shoulder. Their solidarity felt wonderful, but more, it felt right.

"Actually, yes, I did think that." She blushed as she made that confession then turned her attention to their guest. "I'm so pleased, Mr. Paris, that you're not."

"I'd have brought a state cop, Ms. Dalton, if that had been my intent. Our office is, however, interested in Mr. Marsh, and his connection to Frederick Barnes." He looked up, including the men in his conversation. "The New York AG's office has been interested in this person for some time, as has the Federal Bureau of Investigation. As near as anyone can tell, he's usually very careful in his dealings, but he *has* raised a number of red flags in the last couple of years."

So Maddy repeated for the benefit of Sean Paris and his recorder all that had happened between herself and Kevin Marsh. While she spoke, Chase got up and poured the coffee Lucas had made.

When she finished speaking, Lucas filled in the details of his encounter with the surveyors. Finally, after more than half an hour, Paris turned off the recorder.

"Not that you weren't within your rights to be frightened, Ms. Dalton—"

"Maddy, please."

"Maddy, then. But Kevin Marsh doesn't sound like an overly intelligent man."

"I don't think it's a lack of intelligence on his part," Maddy said. "I think it's more a case of the man being extremely narcissistic. As for the being frightened part, my fear began to abate once I told Chase and Luke what was going on."

"We should discuss whether or not you intend to bring charges against him."

"Charges? My goodness, for what?" It had never occurred to Maddy that she could so easily turn the tables on Kevin.

"Oh, let's see," Chase said, his hostility toward Kevin barely leashed. "There's extortion, for starters."

"Threatening with a dead weapon," Lucas dead-panned, which made Maddy snort and the other two men snicker.

"And if he gets nasty, we could throw in accessory after the fact, conspiracy to commit a felony since he did speak to drug dealers and received knowledge of drug deals." That Sean Paris had chimed in told her as nothing else could have where he sat, ethically.

"We'll talk, the three of us, about whether or not we want to bring charges and let you know in a couple of days, if that's all right?" Maddy said. The look of pleasure on both Lucas and Chase filled her heart with contentment.

"That's fine. I'd want to discuss things with my family, too, before making that kind of a decision."

They walked Sean out to his car. Before they'd reached it, however, the sight of a large truck coming down the drive toward them captured all of their attention.

"Well, now, isn't this special?" Chase said, rubbing his hands together, an expression of glee on his face.

It was Sunday, Maddy realized then. And just like clockwork, here came Kevin. She still couldn't believe that he would think she'd actually give in to him.

The shiny new red Ford F-350 King Ranch pulled around Sean Paris' little Nissan and glided to a smooth stop.

The driver's door opened, and Kevin Marsh got out, his tan suit, white shirt, dark bolo tie and white Stetson all looking immaculate. Another man sat in the truck with him, and he got out too. This man was a stranger to Maddy. Dressed nattily in denim jeans and a blue buttoned shirt, his wide smile instantly sent shivers of dislike down her spine.

Kevin Marsh could be an irritant, to be sure. But in this other man Maddy sensed real danger.

His usual arrogance in full view, Marsh strode up to Maddy as if he owned her, not even acknowledging the men with her. Then he noticed the charred debris beyond her.

"What the hell happened there?"

"There was a fire," Maddy replied. Before Marsh could react to that, Chase nudged her.

"See? I *told* you small-dick men drive big-ass trucks." Chase said.

"So you did. I'm so sorry I doubted you."

"Now see here, Maddy. You ought not let the hired hands get too familiar." Then he nodded toward the charred ruins of Lucas' house. "And if you had a *real man* around, things like that wouldn't happen. Now I've brought my friend Rick with me so you could meet him, as he is going to be best man at our wedding."

"Rick?" Maddy questioned. She felt pretty certain that she knew the names of all of Kevin's friends—the few there were—and that there'd never been a Rick among them.

Kevin's 'friend' stepped forward, hand extended, a chilling smile on his face. "Rick Barnes. I'm very pleased to meet you, Maddy. You don't mind if I call you Maddy, do you? I feel as if I already know you, the way Kevin has gone on and on about you for so long."

"That's it."

Lucas's two words warned Maddy he was about to lose his temper. He shot her a look of half-apology, and she realized in that instant that despite his anger, he was willing to step back and let her handle Marsh, if that's what she wanted to do.

Just as she motioned for Lucas to go ahead, another vehicle came down the drive. She had a sinking sensation in her belly as the familiar black and white patrol car belonging to the sheriff's department pulled to a stop.

* * * *

Lucas took a half step closer to Maddy, his attention all on the arrival of Sheriff Barclay. The man didn't look very happy, and that didn't bode well for anyone.

Barclay nodded to everyone then looked at Sean. "Are you Mr. Paris?"

"Yes, I am. Sheriff Barclay?"

The two men shook hands, and then George Barclay turned his attention to Maddy.

"There's no easy way to say this. They found Bill Campbell's car at the bottom of a ravine over in Jefferson County. Near as they can tell, he ran off the road sometime before dawn. I'm sorry, Maddy. He's dead."

"Aw, *hell*." Lucas felt a jab to his gut. As pissed as he was at Bill for having set the fire, he hadn't wanted the man dead.

Maddy closed her eyes for a moment, and Lucas put his arm around her shoulders and drew her close. From the corner of his eye he could see Marsh getting ready to plow his way into the middle of a situation where he didn't belong. *Little pecker always did think he was the star of every damn show.*

"Thanks for coming out to tell us, George. I don't suppose there's any way of knowing one hundred percent that he set that fire." Maddy said hopefully.

"Maddy, the fact that he ran is confession enough." Chase said quietly.

George Barclay nodded his agreement.

"See, Maddy, it's just like I've been saying to you. You're only a woman, which is why you have arsonists and men who don't know their place walking all over you out here. You need a real man in your life. Now, since the Sheriff is here, do you want to tell him something? Or shall we just go ahead and invite him to our wedding?" Marsh's voice came out almost sing-song sweet. He reminded Lucas of a spoiled little boy—which he supposed, in many respects, he was.

Maddy blinked a couple of times, and he could see she had almost forgotten Marsh. Lucas understood she was still dealing with the news George had brought.

Lucas looked at Chase, who nodded.

To Maddy, he said, "May I?"

Her expression cleared some, and she gave him a smile. "By all means."

He rounded on Kevin and took a single step forward. Unsurprisingly, Marsh took a step back.

"One: Maddy doesn't need a man, you little prick, she already has two of us, and you don't fit the definition, anyway. Two: If she did need another man, you don't qualify. Yes, that sounds a lot like number one, but you're so fucking stupid, you need to be told twice. And three: if Maddy did have anything to say to the Sheriff, it wouldn't be good news for you, ass hole. As a matter of fact, she's still thinking about that option."

"She's still thinking about marrying me?" Marsh asked brightly.

"Small dick *and* a fucking moron," Chase commented. "But we've been rude. We haven't introduced you to *our* friend. This is

Sean Paris. Sean is an attorney with the office of the Attorney General for the State of Colorado."

"Actually, it's going to be announced on Monday that I'm being promoted to Assistant Attorney General." Sean said that almost shyly, but his grin as he faced Marsh and Barnes stretched wide and, Lucas thought, looked predatory.

"Sean, this is the little shit head who gave that photograph to Maddy and threatened to have her arrested if she didn't marry him and sign over the ranch," Chase finished the introductions.

Lucas noted that George had taken off his sunglasses and was giving Marsh a hard look. He decided he needed a bit more fun, himself. "Not only that, but he's already made a deal behind Maddy's back to sell her land to—if I'm not mistaken—this fine gentleman right here, Kevin's never-before-heard-of best friend, Rick Barnes."

Barnes was good, Lucas would give him that. He shot Kevin a look that spoke of pure shock and bewilderment.

"Now see here! Who are you to—" Marsh erupted in indignation, but Barnes cut him off.

"Kevin—you *threatened* Ms. Dalton? You mean…you never had the right to speak on her behalf in the first place?" He turned his attention to Maddy, and Lucas thought everyone present—well, everyone with the possible exception of Kevin Marsh—could see the wheels spinning, and the damage control kicking in.

"Ms. Dalton, I sincerely apologize! I was under the impression that Kevin had acted in good faith and on your behalf, because you wanted to sell your land. *Now* I understand why my surveyors were so concerned yesterday. Here, let me write you a check right away to pay for the repair of that fence my surveyors damaged."

"No need. The fence is already fixed," Lucas said. He felt Maddy move closer to him. He thought she might be getting ready to speak up. But rather than indicate she would step in and take over the confrontation, she simply leaned against him.

"Not a very good example of due diligence on your part, Mr. Barnes," Paris said, quietly. "What kind of business did you say you were in, back there in New York City?"

Lucas caught a flash of shocked rage on Barnes' face, one moment when the polite mask dropped and his true inner beast showed. He recovered quickly.

"I'm afraid my only excuse is I allowed my friendship with Kevin to overrule my usually more detail-oriented business brain. By the way," he tilted his head to the side, his smile and tone of voice turning coy, "I don't recall saying I was from New York."

"No? Huh. Must be the accent." Paris delivered that with obvious sarcasm. Just enough, Lucas thought, to let Barnes know he had the goods on him. *Paris can be pretty damn dangerous too, for a kid.*

The tension in the air was thick. Sliding a glance at Chase, he could tell the other man felt it too, and more, understood it just as he did.

"Well, now." George Barclay set his glasses back on his face. A good tactic, Lucas thought, to prevent anyone from judging his seriousness by the look in his eyes "Think I'll go and pay my respects to Miss Verna. Let her know what her nephew has been up to lately. And while I do, I'll have to consider things very carefully. After all, I'm a duly sworn officer of the law, and I've just been made aware of some possible criminal activity on the part of one of Marshville's supposedly upstanding citizens."

Barclay nodded to them and headed toward his car. Kevin Marsh recovered his shock quickly, and trotted close behind the officer.

"Now, see here, Sheriff, there's no need to be bothering Aunt Verna with all this. I was…um…just trying to get Maddy to notice me, that's all! I didn't mean anything by it!"

"Like a bully caught by the principal in the school yard," Chase muttered in disgust.

They all turned their attention to Rick Barnes.

"I had no idea Kevin was like this. I'm very disappointed in him. If you'll excuse me, I'll just wait for him in his truck. A pleasure meeting you all."

When Barnes had settled himself inside it and the truck door closed, Maddy turned to Paris.

"Does this mean you won't be able to go after Barnes as you thought you might?"

Paris gave her a little smile. "Oh, I don't know. I think I've effectively chased the big bad con man out of my state and back to New York City. Success doesn't *always* have to end in charges being laid."

"You're good. I can see why Phil counts you as one of his best friends," Chase commented.

Sean smiled widely and once more he looked like a kid. "Ditto. I hope we all can be friends, too? After all, we have to stick together, don't we?"

Lucas had thought he'd caught the vibes earlier. He hadn't always trusted his own instincts in the past, but he thought that with recent activities they might be improving. No wonder the man had been incensed about the fire. Now he smiled and offered the lawyer his hand.

"You bet. Let us know when you're free. You can bring your partner and enjoy a real down-on-the-ranch cook out."

"That's a deal."

The Sheriff's car peeled away, heading down the drive. Marsh, muttering to himself, scampered back to his truck. He opened the driver's door, and froze. To Lucas it looked as if the man had temporarily forgotten the presence of Barnes. The expression that washed over Marsh's face was priceless—as if he was about to sit down in a big pile of shit. He got into the cab gingerly and started the engine of that big-ass truck.

They all followed the retreat of the red Ford with their eyes. For a long moment no one said anything.

"Oh dear." Maddy's voice sounded strained. Lucas shot her a glance and realized she was trying hard not to laugh. "I don't think Kevin understands just how upset his 'best friend' really is."

"No, he's not a terribly intuitive individual, is he?" Chase agreed.

"I wouldn't worry too much," Paris said, smiling. "Barnes is way too careful and far too smart to actually cause the little twerp *grievous* physical harm."

Lucas nodded. "No, but I expect old Kevin is going to be hurting some." And as far as he was concerned, that wasn't a bad thing at all.

Chapter 20

Maddy had never planned an evening like this before. She didn't know much about all the little fancy touches, all the accents that would make the evening special. At one point, she'd wondered, briefly, if she'd lost her mind. She understood horses and cattle and ledgers. She knew branding and calving and could muck out a stall like nobody's business. What the hell did she know about *romance*, for crying out loud?

A vow, a promise and a piece of paper.

Focusing on those words calmed her. What she knew about romance, was that everyone was entitled to some. *She* was entitled to some, and so were her men. They deserved her efforts to accomplish something outside her comfort zone.

All in all, it had been a hectic few days. The fire investigators had been out, and had quickly determined that the fire that had nearly taken her lovers *had* been deliberately set. Further, in searching the property, they'd found a gas can that no one could ever remember seeing before. It had recently been purchased by, and still bore the fingerprints of, Bill Campbell.

Sheriff Barclay had driven out with Verna Marsh, who had apologized profusely for her nephew's 'indiscretions'. "He'd have come out to apologize himself, but he's had a *dreadful* accident. Fell down the stairs at his house. Several times, by the look of him."

Maddy hadn't known what to say to that. She felt relieved all the bad stuff had ended.

She refused to borrow trouble, or even consider for one moment that there would be any bad stuff in their future. One of the best things about living out of town, in the middle of nowhere on an isolated piece of Colorado was that if they chose to, they could damn well keep the world out.

She wasn't looking at the world through rose-colored glasses just because she was in love. She understood that Chase had likely been right, and there would be a lot of people in the months—years—to come who would not approve of the way she and Chase and Lucas had chosen to live their lives.

So be it.

For the immediate present, neither Pat nor Charlie seemed to care one way or the other how Maddy, Chase and Lucas lived. Chase had said that certainly surprised him. She wasn't certain what he meant by that.

Maddy never thought she'd ever be looking at a happy-ever-after for herself, but damned if that wasn't exactly what she hoped and prayed for.

If nothing else, the last few days had taught her the value of love, and what mattered most in life, and what did not.

So she'd come to a decision. She wanted to do something special for the men she loved. She knew exactly what she wanted to do, of course, but hadn't been certain of the mechanics of it. Her new friend Sean Paris had proven a huge help there.

Maddy smiled. Oh, she'd been sly setting things in motion. She'd casually mentioned to her men that it sure would be nice if they could all dress up and go out to dinner—like a date. Lucas and Chase had really come through for her, and they'd all just had a fine meal in Gunnison.

She'd seen the look of surprise on their faces when she'd pinned a white rose on each of their lapels before they'd left the house.

Now they'd returned home, and she asked them to come into the small dining room—a room she almost never used because the kitchen was bigger and cozier.

"What's all this?" Chase asked, taking in the candles, the champagne bucket and glasses, and the flowers.

"Looks pretty fancy," Lucas said.

Maddy smiled, and maybe they saw the nervousness on her face, because they looked at each other before turning to face her.

"Is this for us?" Lucas asked, and in his smile she read acceptance, and love.

"It's great," Chase said.

"There's more. Just wait here."

It only took her a moment to get the chilled wine and her major surprise.

Chase took the bottle from her as soon as she came back into the room.

"Shall I?" he asked.

"Yes, please."

It was hard to be patient, to wait until Chase had poured some champagne into each of their glasses. Maddy could never remember being so excited.

God, her men were great, the way they each took up a glass after handing her one, and stood silent, letting her set the pace, take the lead.

She hadn't actually written out what she wanted to say, but she found the words nestled in her heart. As soon as she began to speak, her nervousness eased.

"I've been a loner most of my life. I discovered a long time ago that I couldn't depend on anyone to be there for me, to help me—not even my parents. So I learned to do for myself, and up until very recently wouldn't dream of asking anyone for help, let alone standing back to let someone take the lead. I built solid walls around me and had made up my mind never to let anyone inside them."

"No one can blame you for that, sweetheart. We certainly don't." Chase's words, and his expression, brimmed with tenderness.

"I saw the burden you carried from an early age, darling. So, what Chase said."

Maddy smiled. Inhaling deeply, she continued. "I had also decided I would never join my life to anyone else's, and as I grew older, I could never see the need to. I used to deride that kind of commitment. I used to say, 'what's so special about a vow, a promise, and a piece of paper? A vow can be faked, a promise broken, and a piece of paper torn to shreds."

"I remember hearing you say that once. Your daddy had been in a drunken rage, stomping all over you, as I recall, because you weren't interested in marriage." Lucas said.

She could see the memory disturbed him. And she knew his anger was that her father had treated her so.

"Well, I've changed my mind. I know we can't get married, officially. There are a couple of states where you guys could, but there is no place anywhere that would recognize a marriage between the three of us."

"Sweetheart, that doesn't matter." Chase's voice sounded strong, even though his eyes glistened with tears.

"All that matters is what we are to each other," Lucas added.

"All that matters is what we are to each other, yes. But I can take that one step further. I can offer you both, if you'll accept them, a vow and a promise. And a piece of paper.

"My vow to you is that I will honor and cherish you, and abide with you always; that I will be there when you need me, no matter what. I promise that I will let you help me when I need the help, and that I will always, *always* be grateful that you love me. I love you, Lucas Calhoun. I love you, Chase Reynolds. In my heart, you are both my husbands."

"Sweetheart." Chase spoke the word, but they both reached for her.

"Just one more thing. The piece of paper. This is the closest I could come to a marriage contract." She picked up the two scrolls and handed one to each of her men.

Chase had his opened first, his eyes scanning the document before flashing back up to look at her.

"Maddy?"

"You're giving us each a third interest in the ranch?" Lucas asked.

"It's more than that. We'll be legal partners, share and share alike. We'll be each others' beneficiaries, and we'll each have power of attorney for the others."

"The State of Colorado wouldn't recognize us as spouses, but they'll damn sure recognize us as partners." Chase's smile said it all. "You, darling, are brilliant."

"And generous. Are you sure, sweetheart?" Lucas asked. "You've fought for this ranch all your life. You fought your dad who had mismanaged it, you fought years of bad markets, bad droughts and devastating blizzards. Are you sure you want to just give up control?"

"I've never been more sure of anything in my entire life. Will you accept?"

"Hell, yes."

They chuckled because both Lucas and Chase answered her at the exact same time. Then Chase picked up his champagne glass, held it up, in toast. "To us. To the three of us who have chosen each other."

"To us," Maddy echoed, and took a drink to seal the pledge.

"Marriage is a sacrament," Lucas said as he set down his glass. "A joining of the parties involved, taking them from being individuals, to being one."

When he reached for Maddy's hand, she gave it. Chase's warm palm cupped their joined hands, and his words embraced them both.

"I think it's time for us three to become one."

* * * *

Chase had lit the candles, so the bedroom shimmered in a soft glow. Lucas had brought the wine into the bedroom, and turned back the sheets.

Slowly, they undressed themselves. Maddy thought symbolism lived here, too, for they were choosing to present themselves, one to the other, choosing to come together with clear heads and full hearts.

With long, loving kisses and slow, reverent caresses, they came together, three bodies, three minds, three hearts, but one love.

How had she ever existed without these two men who truly had become a part of her? Maddy's heart overflowed with love, with joy, so that she wanted nothing more than to give everything, and take everything in return.

Chase came up behind her and gently lifted her arms, showing her how he wanted her to entwine her fingers around his neck. In front of her, Lucas ran his work-roughened hands over her belly, her breasts. *It's as if Chase is offering me to our lover.* Lucas had done that once, and the act had moved her, incredibly. Now, at this moment, Maddy felt like an offering, for she joyously surrendered to not only their pleasure, but her own.

When Lucas stroked her dewy folds, when he parted her lips and tested her moisture, her dampness increased.

Sliding to her knees, she tasted one, then the other of their cocks. Closing her eyes, she reveled in the absolute knowledge that these two vibrant sexy men belonged to *her*, and to each other. Each of her husbands—for that was how she truly thought of them—handed her a condom, and she sheathed them in turn.

Chase gently helped her to her feet, and together they watched as Lucas laid down in the center of their big bed, supine. Cupping her breasts, squeezing them gently, Chase whispered, "Darling, our husband awaits you. Won't you take him into your body? Let him feel your hot, wet clasp. Let him touch the edge of your womb with his cock."

"Yes." Maddy wanted to feel her lover deep within her body. Chase followed her onto the bed, and it seemed as if she *was* a gift he offered his lover, as he helped her straddle Lucas.

Maddy groaned in bliss as she impaled herself on Lucas, as his hot, hard cock moved up into her, stretching her. Chase's hand stroked her ass, down, around the curve until he came to that one spot where she and Lucas joined.

"You're both so hot," his voice came out in a hiss, and Maddy knew he was as aroused as she and Lucas. Reaching back, she wrapped her hand around his cock, enjoying the sensation of the latex-covered rod sliding through her fingers.

She'd had each of them inside her, but she'd never had them both at the same time. Now, as she undulated slowly up and down on Lucas's hot shaft, she wanted them that way with a passion she could barely contain.

"Please, Chase. I want you inside me, too."

"Then lean forward, baby. Put your hands beside Luc's head and raise that lovely ass of yours."

Did she hear music in the air? A heavy seductive beat resonated through her blood, heating, pulsing with need. She felt Chase move behind her, shivered as the glide of his finger spread a silky substance that would help ease his way.

"From this moment on," Chase said as he placed the end of his cock against her rosebud opening, "we *are* one flesh. We belong to each other."

Maddy trembled as the skin of her anus stretched, as the hot proud head of Chase's cock penetrated the outer ring.

He moved slowly, carefully, and she knew if it became too much, he'd stop. Pressure, heat, and yes, pain sizzled along her nerve endings, licked and snapped along her flesh. Arousal heightened and she moaned, subtly moving her ass in tiny sideways motions, easing his passage into her.

Hot, throbbing, Maddy had never felt so full, so alive. Her lips sought Lucas's, and his tongue and lips savored hers. Then he brought her head down so that she lay upon him. One hand stroked her neck while the other reached down to stroke her clit.

"Oh, yes. *Yes.*" Arousal surged, and Maddy's eager body eased, relinquishing the last vestige of control, trusting her men completely.

Chase groaned as he slid all the way inside her ass.

"Chase, *sweetheart*, I can feel your cock inside her! It's as if I'm fucking you both at the same time." Lucas's reverent words caressed Maddy's heart. They were three, and they were one.

"Mm. Lucas, yes, I can feel you too. Oh, man. This is incredible!"

The wonder in their voices filled Maddy with such a sense of union. She could feel Chase trembling behind her and knew he was being so careful of her. Lucas's hands, restlessly stroking her breasts and sides told her that he was balanced on a fine edge between arousal and frenzy.

Could there be anything better in the world than giving the two men she loved above all others complete and total pleasure? Could there be anything more generous than submitting to them completely?

In that instant, poised on the very edge of rapture, Maddy knew the answer to both those questions was no.

Slowly, deliberately, she clenched her inner muscles and pushed back subtly with her hips.

Chase inhaled through his teeth and Lucas grunted.

"Careful, sweetheart," Chase said. "This is so good, but if you move too much, I'm going to lose my control."

She shivered with those words, shivered in pleasure. Her body had adjusted to the double penetration, and her hungry little clit, which Lucas was still stroking, demanded everything.

She wanted it all.

"Come for me," she begged, squeezing one husband inside her pussy, pushing back against the other in her ass. "I want you to let go and come inside me. Hard. Fast. Together."

"Lord, Maddy!" Chase's curse, low and heartfelt echoed in the room and her spirits soared.

"Maddy!" Lucas's cry sounded just as emotion-filled.

Chase's hands clamped on her hips just above Lucas's. They began to thrust in her, a hard, poetic pounding plunder that exploded heat and need through every inch of her body. On her hips, her husbands' hands met, their fingers linked. Inside her body their cocks nudged and stroked, pleasuring her, pleasuring each other.

Lucas's cock tickled her G-spot, the hair of his groin brushed her clit, and the thrusting in her ass impossibly connected them both.

"Yes!" Maddy's rapture ignited, a hot, electric thrill of sensation, mind-numbing, soul-wrenching pleasure and she surrendered to it, rejoiced in it, as the cocks within her, swollen, hot, quivered and stiffened, as Chase bowed over her, his panting, heaving breath bathing the back of her neck, as Lucas's groaned pleas caressed the shell of her ear. Her heart raced, a hard sharp rhythm that soon was matched by a similar staccato beat under her ear, and another on the flesh of her back.

"Mother of God, they're going to find us in this bed one morning, dead," Lucas said.

Maddy wanted to laugh but the energy eluded her. The best she could manage was a chuckle.

"There are worse ways to die," Chase pointed out.

"True," she had to agree.

It took them a few moments to extricate themselves. Chase and Lucas took a minute in the bathroom then returned to the bed, one on either side of her.

"One hell of a wedding night," Lucas said. Maddy rested her head on his shoulder, while Chase snuggled against her back. His arm enveloped her and rested on Luc. Lucas's arm spanned her, and enveloped Chase.

"This *is* like a wedding night," Maddy agreed.

"And the night is young," Chase agreed.

"This is going to work, isn't it? It doesn't matter what anyone else says or thinks, we're a family, the three of us. Aren't we?"

"Yes." Chase pushed himself up on one arm and kissed the side of her face. "We're a family." Then he stretched further and kissed Lucas, too. "All three of us. Thank you, Maddy. Thank you, Lucas. I'm grateful to and for the both of you. You've made my dream come true."

"I thought I'd die a lonely old man," Lucas confessed, and Maddy felt incredibly moved by the emotion in his voice. "Instead, I'm the luckiest man in the world."

"I love you both," Maddy said, contentment filling her. "I never believed in happy-ever-after, but I do now. Because you're it. You're the perfect mates for me."

THE END

www.morganashbury.com

ABOUT THE AUTHOR

Morgan has been a writer since she was first able to pick up a pen. In the beginning it was a hobby, a way to create a world of her own, and who could resist the allure of that? Then as she grew and matured, life got in the way, as life often does. She got married and had three children, and worked in the field of accounting, for that was the practical thing to do and the children did need to be fed. And all the time she was being practical, she would squirrel herself away on quiet Sunday afternoons, and write.

Most children are raised knowing the Ten Commandments and the Golden Rule. Morgan's children also learned the Paper Rule: thou shalt not throw out any paper that has thy mother's words upon it.

Believing in tradition, Morgan ensured that her children's children learned this rule, too.

Life threw Morgan a curve when, in 2002, she underwent emergency triple by-pass surgery. Second chances are to be cherished, and with the encouragement and support of her husband, Morgan decided to use hers to do what she'd always dreamed of doing: writing full time. "I can't tell you how much I love what I do. I am truly blessed."

Morgan has always loved writing romance. It is the one genre that can incorporate every other genre within its pulsating heart. Romance showcases all that human kind can aspire to be. And, she admits, she's a sucker for a happy ending.

Morgan's favorite hobbies are reading, cooking, and traveling – though she would rather you didn't mention that last one to her husband. She has too much fun teasing him about having become a "Traveling Fool" of late.

Morgan lives in Southwestern Ontario with a cat that has an attitude, a dog that has no dignity, and her husband of thirty-six years, David.

Siren Publishing, Inc.
www.SirenPublishing.com

LaVergne, TN USA
16 November 2010

205138LV00002B/222/P